The Treasure Tree

THE
Treasure Tree

by
MARJORY HALL

Philadelphia
THE WESTMINSTER PRESS

LIBRARY OF CONGRESS CATALOG CARD NO. 66–13640

Published by The Westminster Press ®
Philadelphia, Pennsylvania

PRINTED IN THE UNITED STATES OF AMERICA

For Margaret
and
for Monica
who
from opposite sides of the Atlantic
helped

Contents

CHAPTER 1

The Long Voyage

SHE LOOKED UP at the canvas overhead, white and smooth and curved against the blue tropical sky. The brig moved along the glassy surface of the sea serenely, her rhythmic creaking no more disturbing than the gentle rolling of her hull.

This part, thought Eliza, this day, makes everything worthwhile. The voyage from Bristol to Jamaica had frightened her a little. She had seen ships with tall masts in Bristol whenever she visited the English port which was not far from the little town of Awbury, where she lived. But she had never been on a ship, and had not understood about the terrifying violence of wind and wave, nor that a long voyage could actually mean weeks and weeks of discomfort.

The lesson had not been learned immediately. At first everything had seemed wonderfully exciting. She and Edward had sailed down the River Avon in a small boat to join the *Mary* at Kingsroad, and Eliza had felt superior to the land-bound folk going about the humdrum business of chores ashore, with no prospect of an ocean journey to the other side of the Atlantic, nor of sailing as a bride and with a young husband to the New World. They had coasted beneath the straight and towering St. Vincent's Rocks, she remembered, and she had exclaimed with pleasure at the sight of them.

"You will see stranger sights than those, I promise you," Edward Seaward had told her, his arm around her shoulders. "Just think, Eliza. Before we come back to England we will have seen islands we never even heard of, perhaps, met people who have never once been to England, eaten food that will be queer and strange to us."

For all that she had never been more than a few miles from the small village of Awbury, where she and her two sisters lived with their father, the Reverend Goldsmith, the words didn't frighten Eliza. Bristol, which was so near to Awbury, was a big, busy seaport, and ever since the Cabots, the Genoa-born John and his son Sebastian, had sailed forth to discover the mainland of the New World well over two hundred years before, Bristol had sent ships over the wide blue ocean. The many and varied church spires and towers of the town had been the last sight of home for other explorers too, as well as for merchant ships and privateers and slavers, and had been the first landmarks spied by so many on the return voyage. Strange tales were told on the harbor front of people with red and black and yellow skins, of foods and flowers and fruits that had never been seen in England, of trees with branches like plumes and of sickle-shaped silver shores that glistened in a sun that was hot year-round. Even Edward had crossed the Atlantic once, to Baltimore on the Chesapeake, and on his trip he had talked with sailors who had visited much stranger ports. His retentive mind and his vivid imagination had combined with his ready tongue so that he had been able to pass on to Eliza the bright pictures other men's voices had painted for him, and she had listened eagerly, wanting to know everything that Edward knew and trying to form in her own thoughts the scenes that his mind's eye saw.

Now when he spoke of the sights ahead, she was ready for him.

"And we will have made a home of our own in a place where there are palm trees and brightly colored birds flying about," she had added quickly. Her thoughts easily crossed the ocean and were quickly in St. George's Cay, in Honduras, where she and Edward would live for four or five years. Their furniture was stowed in the hold of the brig, along with seed, tools, provisions, and other supplies, and soon she would be running her own house in Honduras. As they slowly left the deep gorge of the Avon and approached the *Mary*, Eliza looked at the ship confidently. She seemed large and safe, lying there in the channel, ready to spread her wings and take them over the water.

Later, though, the *Mary* seemed to shrink. Still, it had not been unpleasant at first. For ten days the wind blew strongly from the northwest, and the brig, alone in the vastness of an empty blue world, moved ahead at a good pace, but after a while in this tremendous blue bowl the *Mary* became small. When the winds changed, shifting to and fro, and the rains poured on them from a leaden sky, Eliza found that the snug and cozy cabin had also diminished in size. She was violently seasick, as was her dog, Fidele, and she wondered what had ever made her think she was cut out to be the bride of a man who could walk the decks of a brig with waves dashing high over the bow, and who remained obnoxiously cheerful through all of his wife's misery.

Then things changed back for the better.

"We're in the trade winds now," Edward told her. "You can forget your troubles, and so can Fidele. I think you should take a turn or two around the deck — you'll find it horizontal today, Eliza, for a change. And soon we will see land, I promise you."

The fresh air restored her spirits quickly, and when they did see land Eliza was able to stand by Edward at the rail and enjoy the sight of high blue mountains that appeared to rise from nowhere into the pale sky above. Not long afterward they left the mountains behind, and approached a long, green island.

"Six weeks to the day," said Edward proudly, "and there is Jamaica."

Only six weeks since the 30th of October, 1733, when they had sailed! It seemed longer to Eliza. She remembered now how her eyes, surfeited with blue, had feasted on the green of the trees on Jamaica, and how pleasing she found the azure and turquoise and emerald hues of the water around its shores. It was heaven, she thought, to step on firm ground at Kingston, and she found Mr. Dickinson, an old friend of Edward's uncle, kind and courteous and altogether civilized, for all he lived in such a strange land where she was astonished to see more black faces than white among the people.

"What did you expect?" Edward teased her when she remarked on the clothes and fine manners of their host. "Mr. Dickinson was born in England. He wouldn't turn into a wild savage just because he moved from our big island to such a small one, would he?"

Eliza had made a face at her husband, and then had packed a small bag so that she and Edward could take advantage of Mr. Dickinson's invitation to visit him and his wife during the Seawards' stay in Jamaica. The Dickinsons' house had restored Eliza's flagging spirits even more. It was spacious and cool, with polished floors and a mixture of furniture that was most pleasant, even though some of it had been brought from home and the rest had been made on the island of strange but handsome woods. Mrs. Dickinson kept a large staff of servants, and although they were strange to Eliza's eye, because of their color, she liked them all immediately.

It was a gracious way to live, she saw, and now, the Dickinsons left behind and the island itself slowly receding over the stern, she was seated on deck in a canvas shelter Edward had fixed there for her so that her skin would not be burned by the hot sun and the sea breezes, sewing on a shirt she was making for her husband.

This, she said to herself, nodding happily and looking up frequently from her needle to enjoy the beauties that stretched on all sides, this made it all worthwhile, the frightening weeks of nothing but ocean and storm, the seemingly endless torrents of rain, the hideous days of seasickness.

"Doesn't it, Fidele?" she added in a low voice. Her dog looked up at her with his brown-velvet spaniel eyes and thumped his tail on the deck. Even in the midst of her misery, she had always tried to comfort Fidele, who was fully as unhappy as she.

"It's our own fault, Fidele," she had murmured to him, trying to close her eyes to the roof of the cabin which sometimes looked as though it would presently be lower than the floor, with the bunk somewhere between but surely upside down. "It's our own fault, poor little Fidele. We asked to come."

As she thought back on it, a giggle escaped her. It was true, they had asked to come, both of them. When Edward's parents died, his uncle had asked Edward to sail on his ship, this same *Mary* that Eliza was on now. After Edward's first voyage to Baltimore, because he had done well at disposing of the cargo and had taken a liking to the business, his uncle had suggested that Edward take the place of his cousin Tom in St. George's Cay, Honduras, while Tom be returned home to assume control of the business, since the uncle wished to retire. Edward had been pleased at the prospect, but when he discovered it would mean four or five years before he could return to England, he had balked. Eliza had at once suspected the reason why. Although he had never declared himself, she knew that Edward had always hoped one day he and Eliza would marry. As for herself, she had never had any other thought in mind. And when he told her about the offer, and she saw his hesitation, she took a deep breath and said, "And would your uncle, Edward, countenance your having a wife in this faraway place? Because I know where one could be found, one who has been well trained in the art of keeping a home, and can cook and sew. She could even wash clothes, if need be," she added crisply, because not even the Reverend Goldsmith's daughters, poor as they were, had been called upon to perform this lowliest of household chores.

She blushed to remember it, and wished she could forget that she had once been so unmaidenly as to propose herself to Edward as wife! But he would never, he told her later, have dared to ask her, so if she had not taken it upon herself, she would not be here. And since this was where Edward was, this was where she wished to be.

As for Fidele, after the wedding, just as she and Edward were to drive away to Bristol, the little King Charles spaniel had hurled himself into the carriage and into her lap.

"Oh, Fidele!" she had wailed. "Haven't I explained to you that I must leave you here? My sisters will take care of you. I've tried," she said to Edward, "but he doesn't understand."

"Then why not take him along?" Edward's uncle had said suddenly. "A faithful dog, even one no bigger than a pint pot, is a good thing to have at all times. Take him with you."

That was what she'd been thinking of when she tried to remind Fidele that his presence on the rolling, heaving brig had been his own fault. But that moment seemed far away. This day was so pleasant it was difficult to remember one that was not. She could have been in the garden of the vicarage in Awbury, with Edward nearby fussing over their livestock, as he did now. In Kingston, Edward had bought, at Mr. Dickinson's suggestion, two goats, some chickens, and a few ducks, as well as corn, fruit, yams, and pumpkins.

Captain Molesworth had not been pleased when he saw the addition to his cargo, but Edward had smoothed him down.

"It's only for a few days," he said. "And I have brought the food for the livestock."

The captain had said no more, and Eliza, watching Edward scatter corn in the hen coops, had looked with interest at the fruit.

"Won't it spoil?" she asked. "There seems to be so much, for only two people."

"It should keep for a while. In any case, Mr. Dickinson said we would want the seeds, that we should plant them at once. Things, he said, grow miraculously in this climate and this soil. It will be interesting, I think."

At the time, Eliza had thought he looked away from her rather pointedly, but then she decided she had imagined it. She must also have imagined a strained look on his face now and then, that he cleared away whenever he saw her staring at him. The climate, she thought, perhaps gave her fancies. Edward was not the type to brood, nor to keep a secret from her.

He left the coops and went to stand near the companionway to talk to the captain. Edward Seaward was tall and his light-brown hair had been bleached to a golden blond in the sun and wind. His light skin was tanned, so that his green eyes looked lighter and even greener than ever. Broad-shouldered, narrow-hipped, Edward Seaward, Eliza told herself with possessive pride, was as fine a figure of a man as a girl could ever hope to see, and his keen mind and strong sense of what was right, together with his good nature and his ability to laugh, made him well-nigh perfect in her eyes. No wonder, she thought, biting her lip to hide the smile, she had invited herself to be his wife!

She watched him arguing with Captain Molesworth, who was a large, thickset man with a bulbous nose and a dark forehead forever set in the furrows of a frown. She did not like the captain, nor did Edward, but as Edward had told her often enough, soon they would be on shore and far from the captain's scowl and surly tongue. Edward, she saw, was angry. He had left the captain's side and strode toward her, his face clearing as he sat beside her.

"The man's a fool," he said, pulling one of Fidele's silky ears. "I can't think why Uncle keeps him on."

"He handles the ship well," Eliza reminded him. "You said so yourself."

"Y-yes, I suppose he does. Although there are many times when I don't agree with his judgment, and this is one of them. He plans to run to the south, to skirt the Pedro shoals. Just yesterday I spoke with Mr. Dickinson, and that friend of his — what was his name? Farrington? Harrington? — about our course, and they said one should sail between the shoals and the island. But no, this stubborn fool will not listen."

"I'm afraid," Eliza said, snipping off her thread with care, "that the captain does not care for your opinions. Maybe he chooses to go this way because you think it should be the other. Men, they're all obstinate!"

Edward took her hand and gave it a little slap.

"How do you know so much about men, Eliza? All men? Tell me that!"

She knew that she had teased him out of his moment of bad humor. It was usually easy enough to do. He grinned at her.

"How well she knows me," he said to Fidele. "And how equally well she handles me. Tell me, Fidele, how did such a beautiful woman happen to be endowed with brains too?"

Eliza blushed. She pretended she didn't hear him, but she always liked to have Edward praise her. Perhaps she was becoming vain after all, although she had always struggled against it. Of the three Goldsmith girls, it had been Eliza who was the pretty one. Tall, slim, graceful, she had black glossy hair and cornflower-blue eyes. Her profile was the envy of her sisters, as was her slender figure, because they were both inclined to plumpness. For all her narrow waist, Eliza was strong, and that had been the deciding factor in her father's agreement to let her accompany Edward to their strange new life.

"Eliza, although you look as though someone could snap you in two," the Reverend Goldsmith had said, "I know you to be able to work in the house and gardens without showing fatigue. And you have scarcely had a cold, much less an illness, that I can remember. If it were not for my faith in your excellent health, and even more in your steadfastness of spirit, I would put my foot down. As for Edward, he is strong too, and I know he will take care of my Eliza, come what may."

Father should have seen me in that tossing cabin, she thought now, looking up at the billowing sail and the fair sapphire sky above. He would not have thought so much of my health, I'm sure. Just supposing, her mind ran on, supposing I had not come! I would have missed this beautiful day, the delightful visit in Jamaica with the Dickinsons, the prospect of having a home like theirs in only a few days' time . . .

"Liza," Edward said, cutting into her reverie. "Liza, I must tell you something."

She turned and looked at him in amazement. Edward was very often serious, but this tone of his voice was one she did not know.

"Why, Edward! Of course." She settled herself to wait quietly, and for a moment there was nothing to hear but the creaking of the ropes, the occasional snap of canvas, the rhythmic splash of waves on the hull.

"Eliza, you enjoyed the Dickinsons' fine home in Jamaica, didn't you?"

"Oh, yes. I thought — I mean, I realized —"

"You looked about you and saw what our home would be? A pretty plantation, with many servants to wait upon us, fruits and vegetables growing all around, fine furniture and gardens. And other homes, as comfortable or even more so, nearby, so that you and the ladies could call back and forth in the cooler hours of the day. All that?"

"Yes." She nodded eagerly. She had seen it exactly that way. How did he know?

"Well, Liza, I'm afraid I must destroy your little dream. I must confess I too had much the same idea about our life for the next four or five years. But Mr. Dickinson has set me straight. Eliza, he told me that St. George's Cay is not a bit like Jamaica. It is, he told me, a large sandbank, to be blunt about it. The town, which they call Belize, is on the mainland, just across from St. George's Cay, on a river of the same name. It consists of a handful of poor buildings that could scarcely be called houses. And, what is worse, the settlement is surrounded by swampland, fit only for mangroves, which, as I think you know, are impenetrable, or nearly so. Fresh beef and mutton are unknown there. The people live on salt meat and corn, and fish and turtle when they can catch them. The men are away from their homes most of the time, going upcountry to cut mahogany, which of course is the reason for the colony's existence."

Eliza tried to control her expression, but she knew that her cheeks had turned pale.

"Oh, Edward!" she breathed. "But —"

"I wanted not to tell you," he said apologetically. "But I knew I would have to. I should have told you back there in Jamaica, and let you stay there, at least until I found out how bad things are."

"I would not have stayed," Eliza said stoutly. "You know that."

"I suppose so. Heaven help all men married to stubborn women." Then the fond smile left his face and he said, "It is really a very grave situation, Eliza. I have no right to take a wife into it, that I know. Mr. Dickinson was kind enough to say that, if we found a suitable ship, I could send you back to him at any time, and he would find passage for you to England, sooner or later."

"You let Mr. Dickinson think I would take such a course!" Eliza demanded. "Edward! He must think me a very silly woman. And a very poor wife."

"I told him I would have trouble with you," Edward confessed ruefully. "And he knows that your returning was solely my idea."

"Well, I should hope so."

Edward sighed. "No wonder Cousin Tom was so willing to give up the excitement of living in an exotic land, and to trade it for a dull life in Bristol, keeping accounts for his father!" Edward said. "I own it puzzled me at the time. But I'm afraid I didn't think on it quite long enough."

Eliza's mind was busy. She would have to revise all her ideas, but there would be ample time for that. Meanwhile, she must cheer up her husband, who was all too clearly blaming himself for getting her into a situation that would be none too pleasant.

"Perhaps Jamaica looked like a big sandbank once," she said at last. "I'm sure those pretty houses didn't grow out of the ground, like so many palm trees. And for all we know, Mr. Dickinson may have some other piece of ground in mind. Your uncle would not send us to a sandbank to live, you know that, Edward. We have our fine furniture with us, and we have the goats, which will both have kids soon, and the hens and the ducks to give us eggs, and fruit seeds to plant, and we have Fidele. And we have each other," she finished triumphantly. "And that makes all the difference."

He took her hand and looked into her eyes.

"Yes, Eliza, it makes all the difference. I agree with you. Perhaps, as you say, it will not be so bad after all. It has been a year or two since Mr. Dickinson has seen St. George's Cay. Perhaps you are right and things will have changed. Now you see what's happened, don't you? You have cheered me up, and surely it should be the other way around!" He squeezed her hand again, and stood up.

"I must see if some of the sacks we brought aboard are stowed properly," he said. "Molesworth was so indignant about their being here in the first place he allowed the men to drop them wherever they wished. I don't want the fruit bruised or damaged, if we should get a blow."

After he had left, Eliza allowed her face to worry a little. She had thought the "blows" were all behind them. This pleasant sky gave no hint of winds to come. Besides, she must busy herself with putting polished floors and slatted jalousies and the richly adorned rooms of Jamaica out of her mind forever. No, not forever, because she could use them as something to work toward. As soon as she had seen the Dickinsons' home she had realized that the parlor in the rectory at Awbury, or the slightly more elaborate rooms of Edward's old home, would not do as models in the tropics. There must be space, air, shining surfaces, places to put odd shells and fans of coral, windows with shutters to shield the sun and admit the breeze. She would, someday, have a house like the Dickinsons', even if it started with a hut on a sandbank. And that was that!

The blow that Edward had been in fear of did not materialize that evening, and when the Seawards awoke in the morning they found that the *Mary* had scarcely moved during the night.

"Becalmed!" Edward said cheerfully. "*That* will put our captain in a gracious mood, you may be sure! He can't wait to get rid of us and our goods and supplies. Every hour that we drift without a breeze means another hour for him of the passengers he never wanted in the first place."

"Your uncle owns the *Mary,*" Eliza pointed out unnecessarily. For once she didn't mind the calm. It had suddenly become much less important to reach St. George's Cay. The ship was now home to her, and the Cay a sandbank where life was going to be unbelievably difficult. "He has no right to scowl so at our presence here."

The period of calm was soon over. The brig found herself once again in the trade winds, which blew them steadily along. The captain became, for him, almost cheerful, telling them that they had gone south of the shoals he had wanted to avoid, and that they would now turn westward and run straight for Honduras, which, thanks to the strong winds from the east, they would reach fairly soon.

They had left Kingston on Sunday, a day considered by sailors good luck for sailing, just two days before Christmas. On Monday, encouraged by the speed with which they were moving ahead, Eliza had busied herself in the cabin, finding little ways of making Christmas into something special and not just one more day at sea. She also began to pack in a desultory way, thinking that she must be prepared when the time came, for no doubt the captain would wish to deposit them at their destination and sail away as quickly as possible. Edward would be busy supervising the removal of all their worldly goods from the hold, and of their livestock and the Jamaica-bought provisions from the deck where he had stowed them, and she thought the packing of the rest of their possessions should be up to her.

Toward the end of the afternoon, Edward entered the cabin, bending to get through the low doorframe, and looking grave.

"Eliza, I'm afraid," he said calmly, "that we're in for a real blow. The sky has turned as black as your old cat Tabitha, and the wind can't decide which way it wishes to huff from. But whichever way, huff it will. I want you and Fidele to stay below, for a while at least. I've asked the captain to take in most of his sail through the night. In the morning things may look different." He helped her move some of the clothes she had spread out on the bed, and put away the movable objects that were on the small chest and table.

"Make yourself comfortable here, you and Fidele. I want to take another look at one of those hen coops." He looked up at the ceiling a moment, his face intent as he listened. "That fool of a captain. He hasn't taken in sail. We're fairly flying along, and the breeze has quickened. I'll go speak to him again. The men told him we were in for —" He stopped quickly. "I'll go on above."

"In for what, Edward?" Eliza asked quietly. "Tell me."

"A hurricane," he said curtly. "But the captain said it was not the season for them. And for once he is right. Don't worry, Eliza. Stay here with Fidele, and I'll be back directly."

Eliza picked up Fidele and cuddled him in her arms. "Thank goodness you did insist on coming," she murmured. "I could not bear moments such as these, without you to comfort and to comfort me. A hurricane! Oh, Fidele, I'm glad no one else is here. I'm scared to death, and I feel like showing it, just for a few minutes!"

CHAPTER 2

The Storm

ELIZA WAS DETERMINED not to let Edward know how deeply she had felt the news about St. George's Cay. Although the happy pictures she had painted in her mind after her first glimpse of the Dickinsons' home in Jamaica had been rubbed out with one quick stroke, she tried to tell herself that, to begin with, she hadn't expected their dwelling place in Honduras to be much more than a makeshift, primitive house, and that she was no worse off than she had been when she had so boldly proposed to Edward that he take her with him.

"The main thing," she murmured, huddling in the cabin with Fidele in her lap, both of them waiting for the dreaded high winds to strike the brig and send her reeling, "the main thing is that we are together, Edward and I. And you, Fidele."

The dog was trembling, and she realized that she had communicated her own fear to her pet, so she made up her mind that she would calm them both by studying some of the recipes that Mrs. Dickinson had written down for her. "Capsicums," muttered Eliza. "Oh, yes, they were what she flavored the roast pig with that day. Hot and peppery — well, they *are* peppers," she said. "And we thought them delicious, after the first mouthful." So many foods, she recalled with a wry smile, in this strange part of the world had to be tasted, the first mouthful approached with trepidation. Usually, though, everything had been to their liking. Plantains. They looked like bananas but could not be eaten raw. In Jamaica they had been baked and were so good that Edward had eaten more than his share each time they had appeared on the table. And there, in Mrs. Dickinson's fine hand, were the words that would tell her how she should prepare them. Plantains abounded on the edges of this warm sea, and so did capsicums, and pumpkins, and many other vegetables and fruits that would make the salt meat, fish, and turtle more palatable. Limes, of which they had laid in a large supply in Jamaica, were to be used, Mrs. Dickinson had advised her, with almost everything — the juice sprinkled on fruits and fish alike. Salt was much needed in the tropics too, she had said, and they had fortunately brought a great deal of it with them from home. They also had what seemed to Eliza to be an enormous supply of sugar, tea, and even coffee, and of Irish butter pressed into casks.

She returned to her study of the notes written in Mrs. Dickinson's spidery hand. Turtle. Eliza shuddered. As they left, Mr. Dickinson had been most apologetic because they had not served their guests this delicacy. Eliza had been glad of their escape; she couldn't imagine eating one of the ugly creatures, but now, thanks to

Mr. Dickinson's unhappy picture of St. George's Cay, it looked as though she would have to after all. Well, she thought philosophically, it was all part of the adventure and would make good conversation once they were back in Awbury.

A wave of homesickness swept over her. Awbury, where floors didn't move up and down and sidewise and where no one was expected to eat turtle meat! Where friends visited back and forth, and met on the street, and admired new ribbons or bonnets. Awbury might be small, and generally considered dull, but how pleasant it seemed from this great distance. Even Bristol, where the masts of hundreds of ships were packed in so closely that they looked like a stand of trees growing along the street, and where you could walk or drive in a carriage along the docks under their proud bows, even Bristol —

A sudden loud boom made her jump, clutching Fidele nervously. She had tried to ignore her growing awareness that the ship was becoming more and more noisy and pitched with greater violence every so often, but this great sound could not be ignored. Whether part of the rigging had gone, or a sail broken loose, or whether it was just from the force of a tremendous wave against the side, she could not tell, but it was evident enough that the storm was upon them. The next moment the *Mary* heeled over, and Eliza, off-balance because of Fidele, was thrown hard against the side of the cabin. She righted herself, tried to soothe Fidele, who had begun to whimper, and wished for Edward. Perhaps he had been on deck at that moment, and had been swept over into the wild black sea. Before she could follow this evil thought to its logical conclusion, the cabin door was thrown open and Edward stood there. His head was drenched and the seaman's coat he wore was dripping with water. He managed a reassuring smile, but she saw that it was an effort for him. His face was grim, and his eyes hard.

"There's more where that one came from," he said. "Keep yourself where you won't get hurt when she rolls. It's a true blow, and that fool of a captain has lost some of his canvas to pay for being so stubborn. Serves him right, but I suppose my uncle will put another light upon it. Stay here, Eliza, and just hang on. She's a strong ship and she knows what she's about, even if the captain does not. The men are doing what they should have done half an hour ago, and it will quiet down soon."

She looked up at him, braced in the doorway, and realized that he stood there and talked to her quietly simply to give her courage. He wished to be on deck, working with the men, not trying to soothe a frightened woman and a whimpering dog.

"We'll be all right," she said, with all the calm she could muster. "But do be careful, Edward."

"Right," he said cheerfully. "It won't last long. But hang on tight, you two."

He was gone, and she found herself fighting the motion, the noise, the frightening nightmare of the storm. Her attempt at courage didn't take her very far. She had just reached the point where she had decided that since die she must, die they all must, she would rather be at Edward's side and share his fate than to end her life in the heaving, tossing box of a cabin. Since she knew she couldn't walk two steps in the violence of the motion, but would be forced to crawl on all fours, and since she couldn't crawl without putting down Fidele, who would be battered and bruised in no time, she gave up the notion and continued to crouch there on the bunk, holding the dog, which was, she thought, no more terrified than she was herself.

Several times in the next few hours Edward appeared at the cabin door, usually after a series of mighty waves had all but turned the ship keel upward and there was comparative calm for a few moments. He satisfied himself that Eliza and Fidele were all right, and he gave her the comfort of knowing that he was still there. Sometimes he smiled at her briefly and gave her a wet and salty kiss, or a quick, damp hug. Sometimes he stayed for a moment or two to talk. Once he even sat tiredly on the bunk beside her, telling her that the goats had fallen down the companionway but were alive, if somewhat unhappy, that the chickens and ducks had stopped squawking and making a great commotion, apparently paralyzed by fear, that so far no man had been washed overboard, and that the storm was, inevitably, diminishing.

"The door to the passage," he reported, "has in some way succeeded in jamming. It can be opened with the greatest difficulty — in fact, I have had to ask one of the men to help me each time, or I would visit you more frequently, Eliza. Besides, I feel I am needed on deck. You do understand, don't you?"

She nodded. Her strength seemed to be leaving her, and she wanted to make herself sit upright and look alert while he was there. It became more and more difficult for her, but she dared not lie down, and of course trying to sleep was out of the question. The next time he appeared at the door, he said little, but his face was still grim. She found out later that just a few moments before, two of the men had been swept away into the blackness of the night, disappearing like dropped pebbles in the foam-crested sea.

In spite of it all, she managed to doze a little now and then, wedging Fidele into a corner, with pillows to cushion him against the walls. It was the sort of sleep that comes from sheer fatigue brought about by the strain of hour after hour of fear. It was not sleep, really, but an extension of the nightmare in that she felt numb and dazed, rather than asleep. At last Edward came down, muttering violently about the companionway door that was still giving trouble, and for half an hour or so he stayed with her, taking Fidele from her and letting her brace herself against his strong body so that she could relax her tired, aching muscles for a few moments at least.

Suddenly her weary mind was aware that Edward had stiffened. He moved his arm cautiously, sitting up straight, and there was a sense of urgency and haste about the careful motion.

"What is it?" she asked quickly, fully conscious at once. The cabin still rocked and heaved, and the wind and waves outside seemed as raucous as ever, but he had heard something, she knew, that her own ears had not.

"I heard someone call 'land,' " he said. "I'm certain of it. A voice cried, 'Breakers ahead! Land. Land.' " He stood up and was gone before she knew it. Eliza pulled

Fidele to her and waited, her heart beating wildly. For an instant she had thought, We are saved! We have come to land at last. Then she had realized that land, in such an uproar, could mean only one thing. The ship would crash upon the shore. Innocent as she was of the ways of ships and sailing, she sensed that the *Mary* was out of control, and that no amount of skill could keep her from dashing herself to pieces on sand or rock, in this storm.

It seemed hours before Edward came back. His face was pale beneath its tan, and his green eyes were blazing. "The fools. The crazy fools!" he cried. "Eliza, they have taken a boat and gone. The crazy fools."

"And left us here to die?" Eliza in her panic gripped Fidele so fiercely that he yelped with pain.

"We could have gone. At least, I suppose we could have." Edward sat down on the bunk, and even in the midst of her fear Eliza realized how odd that was. Deserted on a ship about to crash to her doom, Edward seemed to have lost his initiative and courage. He could only sit down and look at her dazedly. Then he roused himself. "They haven't a chance of making it, in this sea," he said quietly. "Their boat is too small. One wave will finish it off. I prefer to take a chance on the *Mary*. She has stood many waves so far." He rose suddenly and held out his hand. "We must go on deck and see what can be done. Soon it will be daylight. And at least up there we won't die like rats in a trap. Come, Eliza, we — "

At that moment the *Mary* surged high into the air, and instead of descending to the depth of the next trough between the giant waves, she crashed with enormous force on something hard, and then was still. Eliza staggered backward and was thrown violently against the wall. Edward, too, was slammed across the cabin. With a yelp Fidele flew through the air and landed in the far corner.

"Eliza, are you all right?"

"Yes." She felt as though every bone in her body had been broken, but she made herself stand up. It seemed queer to have the cabin motionless. It was tilted at an angle, to be sure, but it was stationary. She hurried to pick up Fidele, balancing herself unsteadily on the slanted floor.

"Come quickly." He held out his hand and pulled her after him. Suddenly he stepped back and she had difficulty moving in time to avoid being stepped on. "The water!" he said. "Look." A waterfall was pouring down the companionway, but it stopped after a moment. "Here, before it comes again. That was probably a wave. Or maybe it was the last of what had washed over us as we struck. Hurry, Eliza. Give me the dog."

It was the first time she had left the cabin in hours. It had been daylight when she had gone below, and now it was dark. It must be, she thought, about four o'clock in the morning. The night was as black as a night could be, made all the more so by streaks of jagged lightning that sliced through it and illumined the black water briefly. After one of those flashes, she heard Edward say, "I think I saw them then. The boat, and the men. But I can't be sure. The waves are so high." He clutched her arm as the deck moved once more under their feet.

"Come back, Eliza. We must go below again. The brig has pulled loose of the rock or reef, and is going to move." He pulled her down the companionway, closing the door behind them to prevent the water from entering in as it had started to before.

After that, there was a series of thumps and jolts, a severe scrape or two, and then quiet. The waves no longer seemed to break over the ship, but Edward said, "There is nothing we can do but wait for daylight and for the storm to subside. It appears that we have somehow slid over a reef, because it is quieter, and we are not moving, or at least not much. Go back into the cabin, Eliza. You'll be more comfortable there."

"Only if you come," she said firmly. "I've had enough of being alone in that cabin, thank you, and I'm not going to let you out of my sight again. Don't tell me you insist, because I won't do it unless you come with me."

Edward sighed. "Perhaps it's just as well. At least we should brace ourselves so that if the *Mary* begins to travel, or gets buffeted about by the waves, we won't break our necks."

What difference if we did, Eliza thought disconsolately. We're in the middle of nowhere, on a ship that has been wrecked, the men and the captain have deserted us, it's black as pitch outside, and I'm so tired I don't really care whether I break my neck or not. And if I'm tired, think of Edward, who has been up on deck all this time working with the crew while I have been sitting still in the cabin. In defiance of his instructions, she crawled to the cabin, twitched the blankets from the bed, seized the pillows, and crawled back with them.

Just as she had begun to try to create a little comfort for them, the gusty wind started again, dashing the waves with tremendous force against the side of the ship and howling through broken rigging and hanging spars. For comfort, she edged closer to her husband, and he quickly put his arm around her. There they sat, Fidele lying limply on Edward's lap, and waited, trying to comfort each other.

She had no idea how long they stayed that way, clinging together, silent, exhausted. At last Edward raised his head and said, "I'll go take a look. It must be light, and for at least twenty minutes the ship hasn't moved. From the angle we're at right now, I'd say we were stuck on a rock again, but the angle isn't too severe, and the water seems to be quiet. The wind has died away too. I'll go and — and look."

He dragged himself to his feet wearily. Edward exhausted? Even worse, Edward without hope? That was in his voice, the lack of hope. No matter how hard he tried, he couldn't conceal it from her. She knew him too well.

"Not," she said, pushing herself somehow to her feet, "without me. Remember what I said. I'll leave Fidele here, though. Here, Fidele, curl up on that pillow. No, you cannot come. Stay, Fidele. Stay."

The sound of her own voice made her feel better. She was determined to cheer Edward up, and realized that at the same time she was doing as much for herself. He climbed the steps, and struggling with the door, succeeded at last in opening it. A wave of fresh air rolled down the companionway to her, and beyond Edward she saw the first pale light of day. The wind had stopped, and the sound of the waves was only a murmur.

"Oh, Edward," she cried, "where are we? What has happened? Can you tell?"

She scrambled up after him and he reached out an arm. She moved inside its protective circle and looked around. The stern of the *Mary* was secure on a reef, but the rest of her had gone over the rocky barrier and was lying in a calm lagoon. To one side was a beach, gleaming white in the pale shine from the sky, and both astern and ahead of them loomed great high peaks.

"The boat," she said. "And the men. Can you see any sign of them?"

He shook his head. "They could have reached another cove, or entered the reef in another place," he said. Then he turned and looked around and above them, shaking his head in disbelief. Eliza looked too. The ship was a shambles. Masts were broken, with parts of them hanging by their rigging. Other lengths of masts and booms were gone altogether. The boats had washed away. With the exception of the big water cask, most of the boxes and crates that had been lashed to the deck had disappeared, although, she saw with surprise, the hen coops acquired in Jamaica were still there.

Edward crossed to the coops and looked inside. "These have drowned," he said, indicating the coop that had held the guinea fowl and some of the hens. "And these — the ducks and the four fowl — aren't in very good shape. They may be all right, if we can dry them out in the sun. And see, Eliza, there is the sun."

How strange, she thought, that a night could be so dark and violent and tragic, and then the sun could rise upon an ocean as serene and smiling as though it had never known a storm. She crossed and impulsively took Edward's arm.

"Perhaps it's an omen," she said, not quite believing it but wanting to. "The sun comes up on a new day, and we forget the awful night."

That was nonsense. They would never forget it. How could they? But he smiled at her.

"That's my girl," he said, squeezing her arm. "Well, we've shipped plenty of water. I guess I'd better see what I can do about the pumps. I'll cut the ropes on the coop, Eliza. Perhaps you can see to it that the sun gets on those poor creatures."

She nodded, looking at the filmed eyes of the fowl and wondering if a mere drying out was going to bring them to life again. She listened anxiously for sounds that meant Edward was working at the pumps, and all the time she looked about for signs of the boat. Surely the men must be somewhere nearby; soon they would appear and float the ship off the reef, fix up the broken masts and mend the sails. But in spite of her determined optimism, her ears kept hearing Edward say, *They haven't a chance of making it in this sea, the boat is too small.* But some had made it — Edward and Eliza and the *Mary*, and Fidele.

She hurried to the companionway and called to Fidele. He yelped with remembered pain and with new pleasure, and hobbled happily up the steps, overjoyed to be out in the air again. She noticed that he wouldn't leave her for a moment, following her every move with great determination, and she smiled because she felt the same way about Edward. It had taken real courage for her to let him go below. Right now Edward seemed to be the whole world, and without him she felt lost.

At last he came up, rubbing his arms wearily.

"I finally got one of the pumps to work, but the water comes in as fast as I can pump it out. We must have stove the bottom, so there's no sense in wasting energy on it. Besides I feel a breeze coming up, and if it should blow us off the rock and into deep water, we might sink. I think I'd better stay here and try to maneuver her, if she moves. Let's hope the rudder works."

It was not long before he gave a pleased shout. "We're slipping off the reef," he cried. "See. And she's righting herself." Eliza saw that this was true. The deck no longer slanted, and now, as she moved about the ship, she did not find herself climbing uphill going one way, or bracing herself to keep from sliding down the other. "And the rudder is safe!" he cried, again in the same pleased tone. Nevertheless, he scowled as he clung hard to the tiller, concentrating on it and on what was happening.

"We're heading right for the beach, Edward!" Eliza cried. "Is that what you want?"

"Exactly. And look, Eliza, see that little inlet? I think I have enough control over the ship to make it." She watched him as he pushed and tugged at the stick. At one point it looked as though they would crash on a rock, but the current that had taken charge of their progress moved them safely by, and at last the brig moved slowly into the inlet and suddenly, with unexpected force, ground to a stop in sand. The Mary was in a small cove, with rocks on the port side and a sandy

beach on the starboard. The sandy beach stretched
across the bow as well. Astern lay the limpid blue waters
of the peaceful lagoon. Beyond, the island swooped upward to a great height and stretched far on both sides.

Eliza, picking herself up from her hands and knees
where the shock of grounding had tossed her, brushed
her skirts off and looked around at the scene.

"Well, Edward," she said, "I had never intended to
be shipwrecked, nor had you, I expect. But if one had
to be shipwrecked, I believe one could not find a prettier
place."

He laughed and sat down wearily on the deck.

"When I promised to provide for you to the best of
my ability," he agreed, "I had not bargained for being
forced to find a desert island for you somewhere. But as
long as you are satisfied that I have done the best I
could — "

She kissed him quickly. "The very best," she said
solemnly. He closed his eyes with weariness for a moment, and she looked again at the world around her, but
this time instead of the tree-crowned hilly land, the
smiling lagoon, the placid reaches of the sea, she saw
savages who might attack them, fearful sharks and other
sea creatures that could devour them, marauding ships
crowding the sea to seize them and take them into
slavery. The full consciousness of their situation weighed
her down. She looked at Edward, strained and still pale,
his eyes circled. His face was dirty, and his hands almost
black, his shirt was torn and he had somewhere lost a
shoe. But to his wife, who was only a few years younger
than he, Edward, at this moment, had the appearance of

a hero. He was twenty-three years old; he was not a sea-man; he had never labored overmuch with his hands. Yet he had somehow contrived to keep them alive, had used his judgment and had cautiously decided against the perils of taking to a small boat in the storm; he had guided a disabled vessel to a place of safety, had discovered how to use the ship's pumps and had worked at them. And, she felt sure, looking at him earnestly, he would be equal to whatever occasion arose.

She secretly determined to be partner and aide to him, to take what came and to ease the way for him whenever she could. Silently she rose to her feet and went to the water cask, which, although nearly empty, was still lashed to the deck.

Edward opened his eyes to find his wife bathing his face with her own kerchief dipped in water, and she was sure that he didn't notice that there were some tears mingled with the stale brackish water from the cask. She had already determined upon her first rule: Never let him see how frightened you are, Eliza Goldsmith Seaward. That would be no help to him, and he will have enough on his mind without worrying about the state and condition of yours.

"Come, Eliza," he said at last, "save some of that water for yourself. The beauty of Awbury has the dirtiest face this side of Newcastle!"

She smiled at him, making her face set into lines of cheer although it was difficult. And Edward smiled back. Suddenly he seized her, straining her to him in a close embrace. She knew then, because he said nothing and because he drew her to him so tightly, that he was frightened too. He would never tell her, she was sure of that; he would ever do his best to hide his doubts and fears from her. But the tight clutch of his arms conveyed to her the state of his mind.

I asked to come, she told herself, and I will be a help, not a hindrance. We are here. We are together. And we are able to laugh because I have a dirty face!

CHAPTER 3

The Few Days

IT WAS SOME TIME before they felt equal to the task of picking themselves up and taking a good look at the world into which they had blundered. First, although they themselves were later amazed to recall it, they sank into a doze in the lee of the cabin. As the sun climbed higher in the sky, the young couple, their dog curled up between them, gave way to the strain of the nightmare hours just behind and fell into the brief deep sleep of utter exhaustion.

Eliza awoke first, saw that her husband was still asleep, and sat quietly, looking with wide eyes at the island. Ahead and to the left was a promontory that appeared, from the deck of the *Mary,* to be a great mountain, and farther to the left was one that rose even higher. She fearfully regarded the nearer one for some time, sure that savage eyes must be peering down from the rocks, the eyes of people ready to destroy them at any moment. However, no motion was to be seen except the gentle waving of the palm trees behind the white beach. There were many trees, she saw, that were slanting toward the ground or lying flat upon it, trees that must have been destroyed by the same hurricane winds that had brought them here.

In the sunlight, lying peacefully under the shimmer of warm air, it was — if you could forget the hurricane just past and the possible dangers ahead — a pretty sight, she thought with a tired sigh. If the men in the boat should appear around the cliff and set to repairing the ship, she could perhaps enjoy it. Think of the letters, she told herself, you can write home to your sisters. Think how jealous Amelia would be of the romantic incident of being cast up on a desert island. Think how practical Charlotte would ask questions — How did you get ashore? What did you eat? Where did you find water to drink?

Charlotte's supposed questions made Eliza realize she was both hungry and thirsty. The water that she had found in the almost-empty cask and had used to wash Edward's face and her own was not drinkable, and she had no idea where the ship's supply of good water could be found. She did remember Edward's telling her that he had made ready, before he had determined that the small boat would present too great a risk, a bag of ship's biscuits to take along. Perhaps, though, he had left the bag on deck and it had been washed away with everything else. Just as she had determined to force her bruised and aching limbs into a standing position, Edward woke up.

"I'm hungry," he announced, sitting up with a groan. "I am also, by the feel of it, black and blue from head to foot. But I am hungrier than I am aching. Aren't you, Liza?"

"Yes," she nodded. "And thirsty too."

He rose with apparent difficulty. "The hens also, I think, are hungry," he said, jerking his head toward the coop, from which there was now a steady mutter of querulous clucks. "That's a hopeful sign. Well, I hung that bag of bread down in the companionway. We can share with them. And I think perhaps we should go ashore and cook one or two of the drowned hens. And we should bring the goats up from below and feed them too."

"Oh, Edward. Ashore?" Eliza asked doubtfully. "How do we know we won't be attacked? I would prefer to stay here."

"If we build a fire here, we run the risk of burning up the only home we have at the moment. As for being attacked, I'm afraid the *Mary* isn't much of a fortress, Eliza. However, we won't go far, and if you like, we can bring our supper back here to eat, once we've cooked it," he added cheerfully. "For that matter, why don't you stay here, and I'll be the cook?"

"No," said Eliza firmly. "I'm not going to stay here without you. And that's final, Edward Seaward."

He laughed and walked stiffly away, ducking his head as he passed through the companionway door to go below. She thought he was gone a long time, and when he returned he was carrying one of the goats. His face was serious.

"This one has broken her leg," he said. "I'll try to bind it up somehow." The other goat had scrambled up the companionway and stood blinking in the sun. Eliza watched as Edward, trying to soothe the goat as it bleated unhappily but made no effort to get away from him, went about tying up the broken leg.

"You've become quite skilled in many trades in the last few hours," she said quietly. "I admire you. What can I do, Edward?"

"The bag of bread is down there." He motioned with his head. "I looked for a tinderbox and didn't find one. I could make a fire with a firearm, if I could put my hands on one, but that last crash of ours shifted everything around, and at the moment I can't force a door to get to anything. I can use the spyglass, though, if I take out the lens. It will work perfectly in the sun. You might fetch it, Liza, when you come up."

She was glad to be busy, and she suspected that he had given her the chores to do to keep her mind occupied. When she got back on deck, she saw that the doctored goat was lying more or less comfortably on its side. She fed it and the uninjured one some bread from the bag, scattered more for the ducks and fowl in the coop, and saw that Edward had already dropped to the shore and was fastening a rope around a tall sharp rock there.

"I don't know much about tides in this part of the world," he said, climbing back on deck. "Or winds either, for that matter. But one thing I'm sure of, we don't want the *Mary* to blow out to sea again, not unless we're aboard."

Eliza shuddered. "Not even then, I should think," she murmured.

He unscrewed the top of the spyglass and put the large lens in his pocket, picked up two of the drowned hens, and said, "Come, Eliza, let's go ashore." He helped her down, reaching up for Fidele as soon as she was on the sand. "There, doesn't it feel good to have land under your feet again?"

She nodded, but in spite of herself she found herself looking around fearfully.

"Eliza," he said sternly, "we won't go far from the ship, and we will keep careful watch. However, eat we must. As soon as we've cooked these, we'll go back. Then I promise you I'll get out some weapons and anything else we might need."

She nodded again, ashamed that he had caught her. Her first resolution, never to show fright, had been broken already.

"I wonder if there's a spring," she said in a matter-of-fact voice. "I'd love a drink of water, wouldn't you?"

"Yes," he agreed absently.

She looked around aimlessly, as though she expected to see a spring bubbling up from the sand, but the sight of so much unfamiliar territory only served to frighten her, so she turned her eyes back resolutely to the *Mary*, reflecting that having it there at all, and in habitable condition, made all the difference. There, before her eyes, and to assume the blackest aspect of it, was what could very well be their only home for the rest of their lives, whether those lives were long or short.

Unwilling to follow that line of thought, she shivered and directed her gaze toward Edward. He was busy making a little heap of dry twigs and dead leaves, and she watched as he held the thick glass over it, focusing the sun's rays carefully so that soon a little curl of smoke arose. Between them they plucked the hens, and by the time the fire had become more than a flicker of casual flame, the chickens were placed above it on a makeshift grid, and quickly broiled. Fidele liked chicken livers, cooked or not, and had gobbled up all that they would give him before their own meal was broiled sufficiently, and they watched him as he ran around the beach, never straying far from them, wondering if perhaps his instincts might not lead him to a spring.

"There's plenty of water aboard. There must be," Edward said. "And I'll get to it as soon as we've eaten. There, they must be ready. These will not be quite as tasty as those your mother and mine have cooked at home, Liza, but I expect they'll taste good enough to us now. All right, let's go back on board."

Eliza would never have believed that not-quite-cooked chicken could disappear in such a hurry, and with nothing but dried biscuit to accompany it. As soon as they had eaten, Edward discovered in the galley a teakettle that had some water in it, and they drank that. Even this stale water tasted wonderful to them, after their hours of thirst.

"Now to work," Edward said at last. "Most of the fruits and vegetables are in hampers in the steerage, and I couldn't budge the hatch. I think I'm equal to it after that food!" He saw Eliza sitting numbly, looking up at him. "Why don't you straighten up the cabin?" he suggested. "It looked as though everything had slid into one corner, as I remember it. And if you wish to clean up here, I suggest you put the bones into that empty cask. We'll dispose of them later."

She heard him whistling cheerfully as he worked over the hatch, and was ashamed that he had had to tell her what to do. That's the last time for that too, she mut-

tered to herself. Anyone would think she had been
brought up a lady, instead of in a poor minister's household, where, after their mother's death, the three Goldsmith girls had been required to do most of the work
around the house. For that matter, Eliza was considered
an exceptionally good cook, and yet she had stood idly
by, helping only with the plucking of the chickens, while
Edward had taken complete charge of getting their
meal.

"Until the men come, and Dennis is back in his galley
again, I will be cook," she said to Fidele firmly. He
looked at her with his trusting brown eyes, thumping
his short tail in agreement, and she wished she could
share his apparent acceptance of the situation. He yelped
a bit when he moved sometimes, so she knew he had
been tossed into a few aches and pains himself, but he
was obviously confident that they would take care of him
as she must expect Edward to take care of her.

All the same, she thought, looking out over the island
for a moment, I'll be glad when the men come. I'll even
be glad to see Captain Molesworth's cross, ugly face!

Before she had finished her own chores, Edward appeared, looking pleased. His arms were loaded down
with plantains, yams, and another large supply of biscuits.

"Might as well turn out what's left in the other biscuit bag for the fowl," he said cheerfully. "I've come
upon this new lot, and I'm sure there's more below. I
found the water too, Eliza, and vegetables and fruit."
He threw the plantains to the goats, and they ate them
eagerly, even the goat now called Limpy because of her

broken leg. The fowl had dried out and seemed none the worse for their experience, although they still looked a little bedraggled, and pecked busily at the bits of bread.

"I'm going to climb the rigging," Edward announced, after he had made another trip below and reappeared with three loaded muskets and a supply of cartridges. "Maybe I can see more of where we are."

Eliza, who preferred to be separated from her husband by as little distance as possible, followed him forward, and as he climbed he called down his information to her.

"On the other side of the beach there's a great lake!" he exclaimed, and she wondered why this should please him so much. "Or perhaps a harbor. In any case, nice smooth water, with land all around. This is an isthmus we seem to have blundered into. It wouldn't be too difficult to cross it beside that tremendous hill there, since it's flat and mostly sandy." He dropped back to the deck with a grunt. "Want to try? I have the muskets, you know, for protection."

She stealed herself to say yes, but to her surprise found her own voice remarking, "Yes, of course, Edward, tomorrow. The sun is going down presently, and it's been quite a day. It can wait, can't it, Edward?"

"Of course it can wait. I'm a thoughtless brute. And come to think of it, I'm tired enough for two men. Let's put an end to a most unusual day, one that will never, I hope, be matched in our lifetime."

Still, when they had made themselves ready for bed, they found that they could not sleep. The silence of the island seemed to roar in their ears, quite as much as the terrible winds of the night before. The cabin, snug and safe as it had at first appeared, seemed to be suspended in space, a frightening space filled with danger and strange shadows.

Hoping to lull themselves to sleep in time, the young couple began to talk. Eliza started by saying, "Ned, where do you think we are? Really?"

She felt him shrug in the darkness, exclaiming a bit as he moved his lame shoulder.

"I'll find the charts tomorrow," he promised her, "but I'm not too sure I can make anything of them. They're in deplorable condition, stained and torn and scribbled on. There are many islands in this body of water that have never been seen or charted. Although some," he added, in a musing tone as though he were talking to himself, "have been seen but never charted on purpose."

"But, Edward, why?"

"Pirates," he said simply. "Now don't get any notions, Liza. I heard that little gasp of yours. Pirates have been driven away from these waters for more than sixty years, I guess. But once upon a time a pirate ship attacked the Spanish Main, or the plate fleet, leaving the rich ports there and sailing, loaded with gold and silver and emeralds, for Spain. Then of course the pirate had to hustle himself off to some hiding place of his own before he was set upon by his brother pirates. Quite naturally, no one intended to give away his secret to anyone."

In spite of herself Eliza shuddered a little, and he added, "Now, Liza, I told you those days are all over. You remember seeing Port Royal, or, rather, where it had been, in Jamaica? It was called the wickedest city in the world, and at one time pirates like Henry Morgan and the others brought their riches there, dividing their loot among the men but keeping the biggest part of it for themselves, of course. And then sometime later, in 1692, there was a tremendous earthquake and the whole city fell into the sea, and a good many thousands of people with it. A judgment, people said, on the city for its riches and its wicked ways."

Eliza did not like this talk of pirates and of Port Royal, so she changed the subject.

"But here, Ned, where could we be? I know you don't *know*, but where do you think?"

"At a guess, somewhere perhaps halfway between Honduras and Jamaica," he told her seriously. "I have heard talk of islands that would be somewhere on that path, I think. One pair mentioned by Mr. Dickinson, interested me particularly. One was called Santa Catalina, I remember that much. Some English Puritans managed to get charter to it, and they founded a colony there. It was several miles long, larger than the one where we seem to find ourselves, I suppose, and nearly as wide as it was long, while ours appears to be narrow. They renamed it Providence Island, I remember, but in time Spain snatched it away from them and it was then fortified, I believe, and made a sort of prison island. Afterward, as I remember it, some pirates drove the Spaniards out."

"Fortified? Then we couldn't be on that island," Eliza said. "There is nothing here. The fort would be up on one of those great peaks, wouldn't it?"

"I suppose so." He yawned. "And anyway, I didn't say this was that island. Besides, that one was quite a bit south of where we've blown to. What I was trying to say was that there is that one I've heard about, or two, really, and the story has stuck in my mind. I even found them on those battered disgraceful charts of Captain Molesworth's, but as I say, we must be north of them. If they stayed in my mind because of their colorful history, it proves nothing, because there must be hundreds no one ever got around to telling me of. And I think my tongue has wagged me to sleep. You must sleep too, Eliza. There's nothing to fear and the *Mary* won't move away from here during the night. Tomorrow we'll do our exploring, but for now we must get some rest and regain our strength. We will have need of it, I'm sure."

Silently, Eliza agreed with him. Strength they would surely need, in this precarious and completely unknown life they must face when day came to show them the shapes and shadows of their frightening new world. Strength and courage and a kind of confidence she felt she could never find. And in the meantime, sleep, which she was also sure would never come . . .

When they woke in the morning it was cool. Eliza claimed that the deck still heaved under her, after all those hours of buffeting, but she agreed that the long night's sleep had done wonders for her aches and pains, and when, after eating biscuit and some oranges for their breakfast, Edward suggested they try to explore a little, she said that she would go gladly. He shouldered two muskets, gave her a boarding pike to carry as her weapon, and they set out, with Fidele frisking around them as though this were an everyday country walk back in Awbury.

Edward led the way across the sand toward the promontory that loomed so ominously above them, and before they had gone less than a quarter of a mile, they saw a chasm running back into the rock.

"Acacias!" he cried. "And there are several other kinds of trees there. There must be water, Eliza. But let's go on to the top of that sandy ridge. Perhaps we can see the lake I told you about yesterday." They walked in silence for a moment. Eliza, remembering their conversation of the evening before, found herself hoping there might be something unique about the island, something memorable, that would suddenly make Edward say, "Why, Eliza, we are on such and such a place, only a few miles from Jamaica." Surely help would come to them, if they were not far from Jamaica or some other equally civilized place.

"There it is, my lake!" he exclaimed, as he pulled her up a sand dune after him. She saw the surface of Edward's lake, gently ruffled by the sea breeze. He urged her forward, and after a while they reached the top of the ridge. Ahead and to their right the rocky hills were still stupendous, and well wooded far up their steep sides.

Edward pointed to them with a grin. "Do you remember St. Vincent's Rocks?" he asked. "The day we sailed? And I promised you some that would be even more interesting? There they are, Liza. Never let it be said of Edward Seaward that he did not keep his promise."

"You promised me exotic lands and exciting moments," Eliza agreed, "and I must say, you haven't disappointed me one bit."

He started out again toward the rocky face of the promontory that continued to dominate the landscape, and suddenly pointed. Eliza's first reaction was one of fear — Savages! she thought — but it turned to delight.

"Oh, Edward, a spring!" she exclaimed as she saw the grassy glade with a narrow stream running from the tiny pool in its center. They raced toward it, Fidele in the lead, and Edward and Eliza ladled the cool, clear water into their mouths with their hands, while the dog lapped greedily.

"This is the best discovery yet, Eliza," Edward said, and she saw the relief stamped on his face. "Water. Nothing is as important to life as water."

She looked at the clear spring bubbling up so abundantly, and said, forgetting all her resolutions for the moment, "But it is so far from the ship."

"It seemed a long way today, because we didn't know where we were or where we were going. We'll become accustomed to this walk, and it will seem like nothing."

Accustomed! she thought. He talks as though we would be here for more than a few days. Still, one becomes accustomed to things quickly. Father always tried to tell us that whenever we resisted some new thought or development.

At that moment, Fidele, who had been running about, returning frequently to lap at the stream, began to bark. Edward jumped to his feet, cocking his gun, and Eliza clutched her boarding pike convulsively. She felt frozen to the spot, and with fear watched her husband walk carefully toward the sound. For a moment he disappeared into the brush, and returned carrying a creature by the tail. Eliza looked at it in horror.

"What on earth is it?" she asked. "It looks like a miniature dragon!"

"I suppose that's what it might well be," he told her. "It's an iguana. Mr. Dickinson showed me some one day. They are fine to eat, he said, tasting much like chicken."

"Eat!" She shuddered. "I could never eat that scaly, nasty thing."

"Eliza, we must have fresh meat, you know. The salt meat won't hold out forever, for one thing, and then, too, a certain amount of fresh meat is essential to our health. You know what happens to sailors."

Eliza nodded. Awbury was near enough to Bristol so that she was acquainted a little with the life of seamen, and she knew that sometimes after long voyages with poor or insufficient food, they became ill. Their teeth dropped out and their bones seemed to weaken in some manner. But that, she told herself, was after a *long* voyage, one that took weeks and weeks and weeks. She and Edward had had a long voyage too, but they had carefully provided as much fresh meat as could be safely carried for the first part of the trip and they were now well supplied with Jamaican fruits and vegetables. Surely a few more days of their salt meat diet would not hurt them, she thought, and shuddered again at the idea of eating the lizard Fidele had caught for them.

"And what's more," Edward said, giving her his hand to help her up from her seat on the rock, "I propose myself as the cook, just for today. Well taught you may have been, my proud beauty, but I warrant your mother quite carelessly neglected to teach you how to cook iguana. We shall have stewed iguana, *à la* Seaward, for supper. I think you'll be surprised at my great talent in that department."

She smiled and tried to forget about the iguana as they returned to the ship. She felt relieved when he said, "I've changed my mind. We'll save this new delicacy for tomorrow. It's growing late, I see. Well, Liza, we've had a pretty good day, if you ask me. Finding the spring was the best stroke of luck we've had so far."

"Except for having stayed alive," she said soberly.

"Except for that." He squeezed her hand. "Now that we have water, we can afford to be generous with it. I think we should give some to the ducks and the hens — they must need it badly."

Eliza nodded. She was accustomed to caring for fowl and had worried about them. As soon as she got back, she filled a pan with water from the teakettle, glad that she and Edward wouldn't have to drink the stale, odorous stuff anymore. Edward, in the meantime, was building a fire on the sand beside the *Mary*'s bow to boil water for tea. After Eliza finished feeding the goats and the fowl, she joined him on the beach. She found that he had also roasted a couple of plantains, which they ate with great enjoyment.

"I found that sack of corn you brought for the hens," she told Edward, "and another one full of biscuit."

"Good. Tomorrow we might dig out any utensils we'll need for cooking and eating," he said when they had finished. It seemed strange to see him sitting relaxed and apparently at his ease, since most of the time he had appeared to be rushing around doing something, and when he wasn't, he was deep in thought worrying about what he should do next. "And," he went on, "if you find time on your hands, Eliza, you might bring up the fruits and vegetables from the hold. Any that are damaged — bruised, you know, and heaven knows they must be if we are! — we could use up. The rest we should dry I think. You would know how?"

She nodded.

"My education was neglected when it came to cooking lizards," she said demurely, "but I know how to dry fruit, and stew it later too."

They went back aboard after that, and Edward picked up the carcasses of the drowned hens and threw them into the sea.

"They've been around in this hot sun long enough," he announced, "in case you hadn't noticed."

It wasn't until the next morning that they discovered that Edward had made a blunder. Eliza was spreading out the fruit on the sunny deck, and throwing to the goats and the fowl pieces that she considered not worth saving, when she looked out into the lagoon and screamed.

"Edward!" she cried. "Look at the fish. A huge fish. It must be a whale!"

He mopped his brow, and let his eyes follow the direction of her pointing finger.

"Whales don't care much for the climate here," he said, "but I think — oh, no, and I brought it on myself."

"What is it? Oh, look, there are a whole lot of them!"

"They're sharks," he told her grimly. "And I lured them in here by throwing over the spoiled meat yesterday. I had just been promising myself a cooling swim, but this ends that happy thought!"

"But you can't swim!"

"So I can't. There's only one way to learn, however, and that's to try it," he told her. "Perhaps we can go over to that lake we saw, and give each other lessons."

"Oh, I'd never be able to learn."

"I don't see why not. It could be useful. Supposing we were attacked by savages, a ship was standing out beyond the reef and we had no boat. We would be forced to swim for it."

"Oh, Edward, don't joke about it!" she wailed. "It isn't funny."

"I know, Liza, I'm sorry." He patted her hand absently, staring out toward the horizon. "You know, that business of Fidele and our — our dinner yesterday gave me quite a start."

She looked at him in surprise. "It didn't show," she murmured. "But then, it never does."

He smiled with pleasure, and she wondered how hard it must be to look brave and dauntless, for her benefit.

"It was your idea," he told her, "that there might be savages here. I own I hadn't yet thought of it, myself, but as a result we have gone forth properly equipped for battle at all times. When Fidele made such a racket, I thought perhaps the moment had come, and I must confess even our guns didn't seem exactly adequate. Still, Eliza, I believe that since we have seen no sign of any fellow inhabitants — either savages or our own crew — we may hope and pray that we won't. See savages, I mean. It's true, we have no idea how big our island is, but unless we've happened on an isthmus far removed from the main body of the land, it seems to me that Fidele's uproar yesterday would surely have brought them to us by now."

Eliza was aghast. She had not thought of that. Edward saw her white face and quickly added, "I didn't mean to alarm you, Liza. I had in mind to cheer you up. I'm trying to say, in my clumsy fashion, that in my own head I feel better about it. However, we won't go ashore without our weapons, so don't worry about that. We will remain as vigilant as possible." He looked about at her handiwork and said, "Very neat and tidy and bespeaking a fine housekeeper! Oh, and before we feed any more rotted stuff to the animals, or the good to ourselves, for that matter, I think we should begin at once to save the seeds."

"The seeds?"

"To plant," he said. "Over there in the glade by the spring would be a fine place, or perhaps in the cut or ravine that goes back into the rock. We should have fine fresh food in no time — things grow rapidly in the tropics, you know."

Rapidly, she thought, but not in a few days. It would take at least several weeks. Then the full force of his meaning struck her. Several weeks. There was no mistaking what Edward meant. He was trying to tell her that it was to be no three-day sojourn on this sun-drenched island, but a visit that would last for weeks, maybe months. One didn't save and plant seeds if one expected to sail away to Honduras in a matter of days.

She was glad her husband was occupied elsewhere. She would not have wished him to see her face as she translated her thoughts and attempted to multiply her courage. She bit her lips, forced the tears not to well up into her eyes, and looked at the island, so green and peaceful and filled with beauty, and thought, Well, so much for the few days. Now we will prepare ourselves for a stay of several weeks or even months, and we will enjoy it.

With that off her mind, Eliza went back to her duties. At least, she thought, making her routine trip below to the hold for another load, there is plenty to be done around here!

CHAPTER 4

The Small Island

FOR THE NEXT two days Eliza felt sure that she had conquered her own facial expressions, and could therefore conceal from Edward the inner panic she felt at the knowledge that the island was to be their home for an indefinite length of time. She was so busy, in fact, curbing her emotions and commanding the muscles of her face to present a cheerful and calm expression that she failed to observe Edward's own worried state of mind.

He worked as diligently as ever. He whistled, called to her, talked quietly when they rested in the shade to cool off from their labors. But there was a line between his eyes she had never seen before, and twice she surprised him standing stock-still, staring off across the ruffled blue of the ocean. Once he answered her casual question much too intensely, and two or three times he obviously hadn't heard a word she had said. Bit by bit she took note of these tiny warnings, and finally assembled them in her own mind. Edward was worried too, probably far more worried than she, because he had a better idea of the dangers involved.

"You have been leaning on him, Eliza Goldsmith," she scolded herself. She had found that when she felt she must address harsh words toward herself, she preferred to say them to Eliza Goldsmith. Eliza, the youngest Goldsmith girl, had been a flighty thing, not at all the sensible young matron who was called Mrs. Seaward. It was Eliza Goldsmith who had done the leaning, who had not been a helpmate to her husband, who had worried him with her own fears.

"And now," she went on, murmuring to herself as she pushed her way among the boxes and chests containing their worldly goods, "now, Eliza Goldsmith, you are going to show your husband that when you invited yourself to share his life, come what might, you were worthy of being his companion."

She pulled a box toward her with a great grunt, then stood in sheepish silence for a moment. Edward was, by the sounds coming from over her head, clearing away the remains of the wreckage. In the lee of the bow of the *Mary*, near their fire, he had made a pile of spars and boards and shingles that they were to use for firewood. Edward had told her that by the time this supply was exhausted, he would have found hurricane-toppled trees to drag out of the tangle of the tropical growth and that he would, sooner or later, perhaps cut down some others — "If," he had said casually, "we wish to clear a space and build some sort of hut or house where we might in time be more comfortable."

She had thought it one of his jokes at the time. This was before she had realized that Edward was, if not exactly planning for a long stay on the island, at least preparing for it.

She was also doing some preparing of her own. Her present mission below decks was a secret one. She had suddenly thought that perhaps the waves and rains of the storm that had delivered them to this place had found their way to the hold and even into their boxes. The notion had crossed her mind a day or two before, but she had brushed it aside as unimportant, since she believed that "in a few days" they would be somewhere else, unpacking their clothes and the linens and lengths of cottons and silks that she had brought with her. Now she knew better, and she had determined to look at her precious belongings, to get them out and dry and air them if necessary, and she did not want to bother Edward with that task. If he knew she planned to move heavy boxes about, he would insist on doing it for her; and if he left whatever work he was engaged in to help her with hers, he would be forced to return to it later because no one would do his work for him. No, she was going to perform this task by herself. She was going to do a great deal herself. Edward had been taking on far too much, even, she reminded herself crossly, on several occasions, the cooking. It had been Edward who had cut up the iguana in pieces, made little dumplings out of flour and salt and pepper and stewed it all together for their dinner. Eliza had been forced to agree that the result was delicious.

"But you, Eliza Goldsmith, could have improvised such a dish just as well. What would your poor mother have said if she knew you had held back, simply because you did not like the looks of the horrid creature, and that you let your husband take over your duties?" She had gone back to muttering to herself as she tugged and pushed at the boxes, but she forgot her lecturing as she discovered the contents of box after box in perfect order. The corner of one wooden crate was wet, and it should in this damp climate be thoroughly dried before it was shut up in a room with the other crates. She knew that much. She would take out the contents and air them well in the sunshine, and then she could move the box itself, when it was empty, and could probably manage to get it up the companionway, where it could take its time about drying out in the sunlight too.

As she lifted out the carefully folded green cloak a wave of homesickness swept over her. She could remember smoothing it with such care, and placing it on the top of the box. Her sisters had been in the room with her, the sunny, square little room with the sloping ceiling. Charlotte had been teasing her, in her dry sharp voice, about washing her finest linens in a muddy creek in St. George's Cay, while Amelia was lying on the windowseat, her large light-blue eyes fixed dreamily on the ceiling and saying, "But Eliza will wash no linens. She will be a fine lady, with servants and a huge mansion named Plantation House, and people will come to call. It will all be so different from Awbury, so very, very different."

"Plantation House!" exclaimed Charlotte. "Amelia, where do you get these farfetched notions of yours? Really! She is going to a place where there are savages and worse, and she has my sympathy if not yours." Eliza, packing and smiling away to herself, had realized for the first time that not only was Amelia jealous of her — she had always known that — but Charlotte as well, and that her elder sister's acid comments hid a longing for adventure and a dissatisfaction with her own dull lot.

Adventure! she thought to herself. Wait until they hear about it! But that didn't bear thinking about, and she plunged on into the box, lifting from their places her finest dress and cloak, planned for Sundays at St. George's Cay.

"Sunday!" she said aloud, forgetting for the moment that Edward might hear her. "Tomorrow is Sunday. And I know exactly what I will suggest to cheer poor Edward up. Now, how shall I propose it?"

"Eliza!" she heard from overhead. "I think I'll walk to the spring. Do you want to come with me?"

"Coming," she called. Quickly she carried her green cloak and the dark-blue silk dress to their cabin. "Just a minute," she called up the companionway. Suddenly she sensed that her plan must be completed before she told him of it. He might laugh at her and call it a silly notion if she merely suggested that they celebrate their Sabbath here as they would have in Awbury, but if he saw she had gone to all the work of getting out their proper garments, he would know she was serious about it.

She quickly found the chest that contained Edward's Sunday finery, and put the things with hers in the cabin. She was a little breathless when she topped the stairs and found him waiting, but instead of the wry little smile he usually reserved for a late Eliza, he greeted her with an almost absentminded stare.

I am right about it, I am sure I am, he wants diverting. "Shall we go?" she said, almost gaily. "Come, Fidele. I have been thinking for the last hour how good the water from the spring will taste, so cool and fresh."

His face cleared, and he nodded solemnly. "Yes," he said. "Yes. The spring has made a deal of difference, hasn't it?"

"And you were right, Ned," she prattled, determined to talk cheerfully, and somehow unable to stop her tongue from wagging far too much, "about planting our seeds immediately. Mrs. Dickinson had told me how surprised they were at the speed with which things grow in Jamaica, fairly popping out of the ground before your eyes. At the time I thought how interesting it must be to watch. And now we will have our own opportunity. To watch our own seeds, Edward, on our own land —" A sudden thought struck her. "*Is* it our own land?" she asked doubtfully. "Oh, dear, I never thought of that. Is it, Edward?"

Edward shrugged and grinned at her cheerfully. "When someone comes to put us off, someone with a prior claim, I will gladly argue the point with him," he said with mock seriousness. "Ah, here is our private fountain."

For a while they stayed by the spring, sometimes sitting on the smooth flat rock, where they could watch the clear water bubble up and well over from its pool to ripple and cascade down a stony bed, sometimes wandering around under the trees, studying reeds and grasses and delighting in the luxurious growth to be found all around them. Edward, Eliza saw, was particularly interested in the lake that he had seen from the mast and into which the water from the spring was emptied. He had already visited its edge, leaving Eliza waiting somewhat nervously on the ridge.

"It is salt water," he had reported. "Or at least as salt as any of the water here, which seems to be less salt than at home for some reason. We can't wash our clothes in our Lake, but we can in the stream, and we can plant our garden near the stream too, and use its water for irrigation. Tomorrow we'll bring some seeds and plant them. I only hope," he added heavily, "that I can sort things out in my mind properly, and remember what requires what. The watermelon, for example, native to hot countries, requires much sun; pumpkin does not. Fortunately they both grow well in sandy soil. That much I'm sure of, but of course I will make mistakes, there's no helping that. Anyway, although I had at first hoped we had a freshwater lake here, I'm glad it is not, now that I think of it. There must be an opening to the sea, which means we may have, at our feet, a snug and safe harbor."

" 'May have'?" Eliza asked. "How else could the water be salt, Ned?"

"It could be fed by underground rivers or channels," he said absently. "We'll find out one day soon. Besides, it may not be deep enough for the ship that comes to fetch us. This is what I meant."

His cares, which seemed to have temporarily fallen away as he spoke of planting, had returned, and she saw on his face a sort of desperation that came, she was sure, from wondering if he was capable of coping with this unusual circumstance and could manage until a ship found their harbor and took them away.

"Tomorrow," she said slowly, "is Sunday, Edward."

He glanced at her sharply.

"Is it really?" She nodded. "You've been keeping track? It doesn't seem possible that it could be Sunday already. That would be our sixth day here, then. The thirtieth, is it, or the thirty-first, of December?"

"The thirtieth. And, Edward, since it is so, I think we must keep Sunday as though we were at home in Awbury. I have put out our Sunday clothes in our cabin, and —"

Her words were stopped suddenly when he took two long strides toward her and seized her shoulders in a firm grip.

"Liza, you are wonderful!" he cried. "I have been worrying so about you, about how you could adapt yourself to this strange island, and such things as eating lizards, and having sharks swim about the ship. But I should have known better. I have a wife in a million, one who can take some of the strangeness out of this world. Now we will keep Sunday, as though we were at home in Awbury! Oh, Eliza Seaward, this has shown me as could nothing else on earth that you intend not to bend under the rigors of being wrecked upon an island, but intend to bend the island to you."

He kissed her hard. Eliza found the tears brimming up into her own eyes, but she was determined not to let Edward see them. It was, after all, as simple as that to erase his worry, because his worry was all about her, and all she need do was to — what had he called it — bend the island to her!

✧

She looked at Edward the next morning, dressed in his finest suit. It was the one he had been married in, she thought with a hidden smile. Little did they think, on that October day, it would be worn under such peculiar circumstances! The clothes were the same, of course, but Edward himself seemed to have changed. His fair skin was deeply tanned, and his hair had bleached in the tropic sun. He was, if anything, even leaner than before, and beneath the soft wool of the blue coat were muscles that had grown and tightened in the last few weeks, first from working with the seamen on the *Mary*, and more recently from his arduous labors on board and on shore.

Eliza wondered if she too had changed, and decided she had. The hands that smoothed the blue silk of her gown were rough, and no amount of washing could entirely remove the dirt that seemed lodged in the finest cracks and wrinkles in her skin. They were scratched, as were her arms, and in spite of all the care she had taken, her arms and her face had been touched by the inescapable sun and were tinged an unbecoming and most unladylike pink.

But it was the surroundings that were truly strange to the eye, the lush green tangle of the island growth, the feathery tops of the waving palms, the golden stretch of shore, and the menacing peak of the promontory just beyond the beach. And, of course, the expanse of restless, blue-green water, sparkling in the sun.

Edward had, at first, thought they might bathe at the edge of the water that morning, before they put on their finery, but he had finally decreed against it.

"The sharks may still be about," he said grimly. "Since I have had enough sense not to throw more food to them, in time they may get tired of staying in close to shore and move away, but I saw the water swirling about halfway between us and East Island, and I have no doubt but they had found something that they fancied out there in the water. We will stay right here, by the bow of the ship, and wash ourselves as well as we can today. But as soon as possible, Liza, we'll go over to our Lake and teach ourselves to swim, unless the brutes have found that too. Then, when the sharks have gone elsewhere, we can swim right here. It does look tempting, the water is so clear and so pleasantly warm, although it will feel cool to us in the heat of the day."

Eliza felt she had no desire to learn to swim, but it was one of the things she supposed she must do. At the moment, she was almost grateful to the sharks for giving her a temporary reprieve in the matter, and found no fault with the makeshift bathing accommodations. She enjoyed dressing up in her best clothes, but made a mental note that she must never, under any circumstances, wear her fine silk gown ashore, or at least not beyond the beach. Her everyday dress was already mended in many places, because every time they ventured into the tangled undergrowth, her skirts suffered even more than her skin. Her wide-brimmed hat too, worn in the vain hope that her complexion could be spared, was awkward, catching on branches and briars, and sometimes being all but snatched right off her head, when she forgot to hold it.

"After church," she announced to Edward, "I am going to change my dress."

"Yes," he nodded. "And I will put on my other garb again. Still, Liza, I think we should walk about quietly, and not return to our everyday tasks. Do you agree?"

They improvised a little church service, and after sitting quietly in the shade for an hour or so, changed their clothes. Eliza, who had spent considerable time worrying about her wardrobe, knowing it quite impractical for her present mode of life, decided the time had come to devise a more suitable costume. She changed, therefore, into a short bedgown made of sprigged dimity, both cool and comfortable. It would, she knew, let her move with greater ease through the closely grown tropical plants. The dress was immodestly short, because it reached only to a spot just below the calves of her legs, and she wondered if perhaps Edward would reprove her, but she had seen a shadow of impatience on his face so many times when he had had to return to her and free her from a sharp point or a rough surface. Perhaps he would, under the circumstances, condone this heathen dress. She looked at herself doubtfully. The skirt, in addition to being short, was slim and straight. She had tied a long shawl about her waist, letting the ends hang down front and back, and she wished she dared tie them together to make trousers of her skirt, but she felt she had departed far enough from the suitable garb of a young English lady, and decided to leave things as they were.

Next she turned her attention to her hat. The broad brim, so stylish and becoming at home, had at first seemed heaven-sent since it would shade the hot sun from her face, but it too had proved troublesome. She caught up a length of muslin and a strip of red bunting from a box of odd bits of material that she had brought with her, and contrived a sort of turban by twisting them together. Then, taking a deep breath, she left the cabin and hesitantly joined her husband on the deck.

Edward's first reaction was a look of amazement, followed by a shout of laughter. Eliza stopped still in her tracks. She knew that her appearance was odd, no one knew that better, but she hadn't thought to present such a comical figure as Edward seemed to think hers to be.

"Capital!" he said at last, sobering as he saw her face. "That's a very sensible departure, Liza, and I commend you once again. Your skirts were beginning to take up more of my time than the island itself. And what's more, Mrs. Seaward, that is a most becoming costume. You look like a Turkish lady, perhaps, or some other Asian noblewoman."

"You — don't mind?" she asked timidly. "The skirts were, as you say, a trial to us both. And so badly torn that soon I will be able to find nothing left to mend, I'm afraid. But, oh dear, Edward, what would Charlotte say?"

"Who cares what Charlotte would say!" he said abruptly. "Charlotte is not here to say anything. Thank heaven for that, too, because enduring Charlotte under circumstances such as these, would not be my idea of the way life should be arranged, not for a moment."

Eliza giggled.

"Seriously," she said, "if you don't approve, I'll not wear this outlandish outfit again. I put it on on Sunday because — because —" She hesitated, saw that he was waiting for her to finish, and added lamely, "because

Sunday seems more personal and private, somehow. Even here, where there is no one to see us any day of the week!"

"I think I understand." He took her hand and smiled down at her warmly. "And of course I don't want you to change. I approve wholeheartedly — I even *like* you in that mode of dress. If it distresses you, Eliza, we will think of it as a costume for a fancy-dress ball. And soon we will both be so accustomed to it we won't think twice about it. Now, Mrs. Seaward, shall we walk?"

Because it was Sunday, Edward had decided not to take his muskets, and it was almost possible to forget the pistols he had tucked into his waistband. They each had a staff, which seemed more cane than weapon, and they walked slowly, arm in arm, enjoying the peace and quiet of their island, and content not to be working at their many varied tasks for once, but just sauntering together as they had long ago seen Edward's father and mother, and, until her mother's death, Eliza's own parents, on every fine Sunday in Awbury.

"Your costume changes have started my mind on a whole new track," Edward said, after they had struggled along for a few yards in the soft sand. "Come down nearer the water's edge, Liza. The sand is packed more firmly there. You see, since we're forced to cross this stretch of beach every time we leave our home, we must devise some way to keep the sand out of our shoes. I have been wondering if we couldn't fashion outer boots of some kind. It's clear enough we can't stop every minute or two and empty this annoying sand from our shoes, since they fill up again with the next step."

"Why not make boot tops out of canvas," Eliza suggested, "to fit over our shoes somehow? There are many pieces lying about on deck still. Unless you think they can be sewn back into sails again."

"They certainly cannot," he told her. "I had twice started to throw them overboard, but I have some kind of instinct that tells me to throw nothing away here, because we never know what we may need next. I think your suggestion is an excellent one. It won't be easy, and I doubt if canvas boots will ever become fashionable and popular at Court, but I think that is the perfect solution." They had reached the narrowest point of sand on the beach, and he took Eliza's elbow to steer her across. "I know where there is a box that has in it a couple of sailmaker's needles, some of his sewing twine, and that big thimble sort of thing he uses — I think it's called a palm. We'll find that when we get back home, and perhaps we can work out how to go about making them."

Eliza smiled happily. As long as she had definite tasks set for herself she found that she had neither time nor inclination to be homesick, and she was beginning almost to enjoy the challenges to their ingenuity that the island presented. Edward, leading the way to cut at the brush, or walking at her side when the path was clear, seemed to be propelling them toward the steep slope of the promontory, and Eliza went along, docilely enough, enjoying her freedom from a wide skirt and the oppression of the cumbersome hat.

"Since we are not a young farm couple today, looking for places to plant and cultivate, or for food, or performing any other workaday task," Edward said at last, "and since we are out for our Sunday stroll, it does not seem amiss to do a bit of leisurely exploring. I must confess I want to get a better look at our world than we've had before. If it doesn't prove too difficult, perhaps we can climb to the top of the Hill, and have a good view of our dominion."

Edward, she had discovered, liked to give names to things. The promontory that loomed above them, and that was always in their sight and thoughts, he had called the Hill, with the even larger height to the south named the Mountain. The island astern of the *Mary,* which cut off the morning light from their cabin, was East Island. The rising, sandy land across the isthmus was the Ridge, and the landlocked harbor was still the Lake, even though he had found that it was not a lake after all.

At first as they strolled along the margin of sand, they found shells of such beauty that Eliza hurried from one to another, looking with rapture at their shapes and many colors and exclaiming over the high polish that was hard and mirrorlike on so many.

"See this, Ned — it's so brown and speckled. And the inside of this — did you ever see such a delicate pink? And this is shaped just like a trumpet, while this one curls like a rosebud carved in pink marble."

At first Edward good-naturedly put them in his pockets, but finally he protested.

"We'll leave these here in a heap, out of reach of the waves, and come back another day with a basket," he suggested. "And I'm sure there will be pretty shells for you to fall in love with for as long as we're here."

"Oh, Ned," she said sheepishly, "I never thought.

I've been loading you down like a farm horse, haven't
I? I'm sorry."

He had put down his burden, and led her away from
the water's edge, still teasing her about her shells, and
before long they found themselves walking through the
recession in the rock that they had seen before. Passing
by the acacias and the other trees that were unlike the
rest on the island, they had reached what was all new
territory for both of them. Fidele, who had been rushing around as usual, had disappeared into the thicket,
and they suddenly heard him barking furiously.

Edward called to him, saying to Eliza with a smile,
"You must teach your dog manners, Liza. He shouldn't
create such an uproar on the Sabbath, you know." He
called again, and then said with a puzzled frown, "I
never heard him bark so steadily."

"Wh — what do you suppose he's found?" Eliza asked,
furious with herself for the quaver in her voice.

"Another iguana, I imagine," he told her. He put up
his hand to silence her, so that he could listen. "Why,
it's an echo we hear," he said. "He must be up against
a wall of rock, or something of the kind." Almost immediately there was a rustle ahead of them and Eliza
clutched her husband convulsively as an iguana rushed
across their path. He was, if anything, larger and more
hideous than the first had been, and even Edward was
surprised into immobility for a moment, but Fidele tore
out of the brush and captured the animal, killing him
expertly at once.

"Well done, Fidele," Edward said, patting the panting
little dog affectionately. "Well done. We'll leave him
where he is while we continue our walk."

The going became worse, and their progress was slow, but finally they edged their way to a clearing of sorts, and discovered on the other side of it what looked like the mouth of a cavern. Edward threw Eliza a pleased look, and for the moment appearing to forget all about her, plunged into the opening, which was as big as a large gate.

"Eliza! Come here!" he called, and she negotiated the last of the tangle and hurried to his side. The cavern, which had looked dark from the outside, proved to be fairly light, and she saw at once, even before he pointed it out to her, an opening on the far wall that appeared to be three or four feet across and at least thirty feet above the floor of the cave.

"Oh, Edward!" she exclaimed, looking around in wonder. From the roof of the cave hung long, pointed icicle-shaped things that gleamed in the few rays of sunlight issuing from the opening above, faintly topaz, rose-colored, frosty white. From the floor rose similar formations. Some pigeons flying about overhead were frightened by the voices of the newcomers. They made for the opening and disappeared in a blue fluttering cloud, leaving the Seawards in silence once again.

"It's — it's beautiful!" she said. "The colors. They look like crystals, those things. They sparkle so when the sun strikes them. If only there was more light and we could see them better!"

"Those are stalactites," he said, pointing to the roof. "And those that grow upward from the ground are stalagmites. Uncle Timothy has some in his office, brought him by one of the ships that visited Somers Islands. They are formed by the dripping water from the

roof of the cave, and the water carries with it minerals of
one kind or another. It is the mineral that determines
the color. I don't know how many centuries it takes to
form a stalagmite such as that big fellow there, but
several, I daresay. Well, Eliza, we must turn back, I suppose."

"But we haven't seen the top of the Hill," she protested, "and that was what we set out to do."

"We won't see it from this direction," he told her.
"This cave is set into solid rock, and we couldn't scramble up this rock face no matter how hard we tried. I
think perhaps we have seen enough for today anyway.
We came by a different route, of course, but not far
from us is our spring. I think this cave will be important
to us, Liza. For one thing, since we've hacked away some
of the brush, it is easy to get to, or will be when I've
done a proper job. For another, it is close to our spring,
and by the spring we will be planting our seeds, so that
in effect, the main body of our action will be concen-
trated here. I think perhaps we can use this cave for
storage. It is dry and cool, as you see, and our fruits and
vegetables will keep longer in the cool air. I'm not sure
yet, but perhaps we can bring our livestock up here. I'll
make a sort of run for the hens, although I don't think
we need to close them up, since they will remain where
the food is. The goats — and the hens too, for that matter — can stay in the shade of the cave when the sun is
high. I'm not sure but that the goats and the hens are
going to live in more comfort than we. Perhaps we
should move ourselves into the cave, instead of our livestock!"

"What about the ducks?" Eliza asked.

"We'll leave them on the brig for the present. If they find their way to the sea, they may swim away and we will have no more ducks," he suggested. "Later I believe we can clip their wings, and leave them by the brook, where I'm sure they'll be perfectly happy. Now, let us go home."

They were silent as they picked their way along the path, but as soon as they were free of the reaching, entangling thorns, Eliza slipped her arm through Edward's.

"Ned," she began, "if what you say is true — about the spring and the cave becoming the important part of our world, I wonder if it would be possible to — But no, it would only make more work for you."

"Possible to do what? And let me be the judge of the work," he said teasingly. "Out with it, Liza."

"Well, you will be moving back and forth between the brig and — and where we were," she said hesitantly. "And — I know it is silly of me, but I still cannot endure the thought of having you out of my sight, for even a minute. There are a great many things I could be doing, much more important to us both than my tagging along with you every minute just because of my childish fears. So I wondered if perhaps you couldn't put a tent, or a canvas shelter of some sort, up there on our Ridge. If I sat there, I could see you at all times, and I wouldn't interfere with your work and I wouldn't — worry," she finished.

Edward put his arms around her shoulders and hugged her.

"That is another of your very sound ideas," he said. "We'll do it at once. You forgot one very important part of the plan though, Eliza. It will enable me to see *you* at all times too. And knowing where you are and that you are safe will make my work easier. And besides that, just looking at you always makes me happier, Eliza."

She smiled at him gratefully.

"Some other day," she said, "we will climb the Hill and take a look at our dominion, as you called it. Do you suppose it is a big island, Edward?" Then she chuckled. "Oh, Edward, so many times we have walked together on a Sunday in Awbury, and you have discussed England and Spain and France and the Americas, and how many times I have heard you say, 'Of course, England is but a small island.' " She slipped her arm through his as they paced slowly along, as they had time after time in Awbury. In the still air at home, she had so often heard him say it, and she had thought fondly that it stamped him as a man of the world, a traveler who had seen other lands. Only if one had never left England, or even some little part of it, could one think of the country as large.

No, England was small, Edward had said so, a small island. And now for all they knew, their whole world consisted of the stretch of shores and the jagged mountain peaks that they could see from the sandy ridge above the *Mary*.

"So now, sir," she went on, her lips smiling but her eyes suddenly shining with tears, "you must revise your views. Because certainly we are *really* on a small island."

"And alone on it, and it is our own," he said gravely. "What a strange thought that is, Eliza Seaward. Just you and me and Fidele, and our own small island."

CHAPTER 5

Eliza's Tent

THEIR FIRST SUNDAY on the island marked a turning point for them both, Eliza decided. Edward worried less about her and could spend all his thought and energy on providing for the needs of their daily life, and she herself, having discovered the joys of contributing to their mutual happiness, could plunge more deeply into helping him in every way she could, spiritually as well as physically. She was ashamed that she had never before looked on Edward as a person who, like herself, could sometimes use a little encouragement, and she determined never again to let herself fall into the position of one who was forever taking, when she could be giving.

Their first move was to take the livestock from the *Mary* to the cave. The hens were carried in a sack, a trip which they protested only mildly. As soon as they were released, they began to peck at the bruised corn Eliza scattered for them on the earth floor of the cave. A pan of water was put near the opening, and it was plain enough that the hens and the rooster were ready to settle in their new home as soon as they saw it. Edward, carrying the lame goat and herding the other before him, added them to the family of poultry, tossed some plantains on the ground before them and regarded the results with satisfaction.

"I think our family is fairly adaptable," he said cheerfully. "Quite as much as we are ourselves, I believe. I doubt very much if any of them will stray away. They have everything they need right here. After a while we may not have to provide food for them, because in time they'll find out what they can eat growing around the cave. This was our second stroke of luck, Liza. First the spring, and now a fine cave. Tomorrow I'll begin your tent, but first let's make those gaiters. I refuse to march back and forth across the beach, my shoes filling with sand every few steps."

Eliza found the work with the pieces of canvas, the curved sailmaker's needle, and the clumsy palm very difficult, but she stitched away as diligently as she could, allowing Edward to take the work from her occasionally, so that she could rest her stiff fingers. When he was not relieving her, he was cutting the heavy canvas and sorting the smaller pieces for eventual use. They were seated on the deck of the *Mary,* in the shade of the deck house, and every now and then they paused in their work and looked around them at the beauty of their world.

"It's New Year's Day," Eliza said once. "Had you thought of that, Edward? January the first, 1734. I wonder where next New Year's Day will find us."

Her husband shot her a sharp look, but apparently satisfied himself that there was no morbid fear in her question, so he answered lightly, "Who knows, Eliza?

St. George's Cay, most probably. Or perhaps — back in Jamaica, or . . ."

"Ned, I don't understand," Eliza said. Her hands were idle for the moment, and she let them fall in her lap. "Why is it that we never see a ship? Just at first you used to say sometimes, 'When we spy a sail' or 'When a ship comes to pick us up,' but I notice you don't mention it anymore."

"I suppose," he said, scowling as he punched hard at the stubborn needle, "that I have, without realizing it, come to the belief that we are well off the usual shipping routes. We should not have been on the course we were on anyway, you know, although that fool of a captain wouldn't listen to reason. And we blew here, actually, although how far off our course we were blown I have no way of knowing."

"Doesn't anyone ever come to this island?"

"We don't know what island it is," Edward said gently. "I have looked over the charts in Captain Molesworth's cabin often enough, but I am not enough of a navigator to make much out of them. The sea that lies between North America and the Spanish Main is a largish body of water and well sprinkled with islands, great and small. And without doubt there are many that have never appeared on the charts because they are as yet undiscovered."

"Then perhaps we have discovered one!" Eliza exclaimed. "That's what we should call it, Undiscovered Island."

"Except that we have discovered it. I have been thinking a good deal about this very point, Eliza, and I believe, when we get back to England and petition the King, as we must do, I imagine, to get legal possession, we should ask him to bestow upon it the title of Seaward's Island. How does that strike you?"

"Seaward's Island. But of course!" Eliza cried. "Just think how it will look on the maps, along with the others." She took the canvas from him and picked up the needle. "But, Edward, if we are not where ships are bound to pass, how will anyone ever find us?"

"If we were blown here by an ill wind — "

"It was not an ill wind," Eliza interrupted, looking about her with a proprietary air. "I mean, an *ill* wind would never have deposited us in so fair a place!"

"All right, then we were blown here by a wild wind — you must admit to that much, Liza. And so might someone else be one day."

"We can't — I mean you can't — I mean, there is no chance of our ever sailing away from here on the *Mary?*"

"I have been over her from bow to stern a good many times," he said. "If we could succeed in floating her, and I don't see how we could, although twenty men might be able to, perhaps, but even if we could, we have not enough whole canvas to make a single decent sail. And although she behaved very nicely when we brought her aground, I doubt she would allow the rudder to have too much influence on her in the open water. No, Liza, the *Mary* is here to stay, for a while at any rate, and we should thank our stars that she is providing us with a home at least. There, is that the last of them? Let's try on our new boot tops, and see how they look."

They were presently doubled over with mirth as they looked at themselves with their legs encased in the clumsy crude canvas gaiters, but there was no doubt about the fact that these new contraptions would work, and at last they could walk on the beach free from the sharp sand that had persisted in filling their shoes with every few steps. The canvas would prevent thorns from scratching or tearing at their legs, too, Eliza thought. She looked down at herself with something like dismay. The short, straight bedgown tied at the waist and the clumsy canvas gaiters topped off by the twisted turban on her head, which of course she could not see — how odd she must look. To think it had all happened to her in a single week! If they should remain on the island for a month or two months, what sort of savage would she appear then?

Edward had evidently been doing his own share of thinking, because after they had visited the livestock in their new home and fed them again, he said, "Let's go over to the ridge, Eliza. I have had some thoughts about your tent." He led the way, and as soon as they reached the spot he began to pace thoughtfully and methodically. The site he had chosen was a clearing only five or six yards from the cave, and about forty feet from the sheer steep wall of the cliff. Eliza, watching him pace and stop here and there to push a stick into the soft earth, could contain her curiosity no longer.

"But, Ned, we couldn't have a tent as large as that. We haven't that much canvas."

"Twelve feet on each side," he murmured, nodding his head slowly. Then he looked at her and grinned.

"Your tent," he said happily, "has become a palace. Of planks, and only twelve feet square, to be sure, but in some ways it will seem like a palace to us, I fancy, after the cabin on the *Mary*, which has been our home for so long."

Eliza stared at him. "Really!" she exclaimed. "But, Ned, so much work for you — and what you don't need, at the moment, is more work — just so I can sit in the shade and watch you toiling away. Oh, no, Edward Seaward, I won't let you embark on one more huge project. You've more than enough on your hands as it is."

"To begin with, I'm not thinking of it as a place for you to sit in the shade, Liza. At least not only that. By this time we're reasonably sure we're alone in this island paradise, which means there's no real reason why we can't live ashore, if we choose to. And there are a good many reasons for choosing to. As for the work, well, I have a plan that will make it a very easy task, and take only a few hours. We have the time to spare, Eliza. We're not going anywhere, not for quite a while." He saw from her face that perhaps he had said the wrong thing, so he put his arm around her quickly and added, "We can leave the house unfinished if a sail appears over the horizon, Eliza. And besides, I have a personal theory about our lives here, at this moment. We must plan, we must keep busy, we must somehow manage to grow. I don't mean we, ourselves, but our world must grow and improve. Your father told me once that idleness was one of the great evils of the world and I am sure he was right. I've thanked him many times for the sermon."

"I'm sure Father wasn't delivering a sermon to you," Eliza said quickly. "I've never seen you idle for more than a minute or two at a time. You're always bustling around doing something. And here — "

"And here, there is plenty to do!" he finished for her. "You're not exactly a lily-of-the-field yourself, Eliza Seaward. I'm lucky to have you."

Eliza found that she didn't trust her voice at the moment, so she said nothing. In one awful flash, she had a picture of what their life on the island could have been like if Edward had been anything other than the man he was. His industry and resourcefulness had made their days there not only bearable but actually pleasant, and his courage and unfailing good humor had kept her from brooding over their strange fate and, except for occasional moments, from being homesick.

"If you're sure it isn't going to add too much to your day's work," she said at last, reluctantly, "go ahead, Edward. But please promise you won't break your back over it. As you say, we have plenty of time," and she was amazed to see how coolly she could say the words.

"I promise. There are so many loose planks on the ship, and around it where I've thrown them off, that the material itself is no problem. I've got to put them somewhere, so why not in a pile that happens to look something like a house," he said cheerfully.

The next day he began his new project. At first Eliza tried to assist him, but finally he convinced her that she was more a hindrance than a help, and he persuaded her to content herself with feeding the goats and chickens, and to do some mending nearby while he worked. She looked at him almost with awe, as she saw how easily he went about this unfamiliar task. His plan was a simple one. First he placed planks on the level ground, side by side, to form a floor. Then he crossed the ends of the planks with others, crossing their ends with still more, and quite rapidly the walls of their "tent" began to rise.

"This would never do in Awbury," he said, pausing beside her to rest for a moment. "A little too airy for our English climate, I'm afraid. But the spaces on all sides will let the tropical breezes right through our palace, and breeze is almost as important as shade here."

"How on earth did you know how to do that, Ned?" she asked, her sewing in her lap and her hands idle.

"I once saw a small model of an American log cabin," he told her with a grin. "It was made exactly this way, except with round logs instead of planks. Little did I think when I looked at it that someday having seen it would prove very useful."

"You," said Eliza, picking up the shirt and stabbing at it with her needle, "seem to store everything up in your head as a squirrel stores nuts. When Charlotte and Amelia teased me about our Plantation House, they did not foresee that you would build it with your own hands."

"Plantation House? What is that? You haven't told me about it," he said, settling back against a pile of planks.

She saw that if she talked to him, he would sit there and listen, and therefore not return to his labors too soon. So she smiled mysteriously, and said, "Oh, it was

just talk, really. You know my sisters. Amelia was having one of her fantasies, seeing us as lord and lady of
the manor. You know how she goes on about things.
And Charlotte was being cross about it, as usual."

"But Plantation House? What gave them that name?"

"I don't remember — oh, yes, of course I do. How
could I forget? Do you remember that very thin waspish
woman who took a house in Awbury one summer? It
was the Northey house, out on the road by the river.
She had thought to buy it, but moved in to discover
whether or not she would like the place and the people.
Most of all the people."

Edward shook his head.

"Well, no, I think you wouldn't know. That was the
year you went to work for your uncle in Bristol, just
before he sent you to Baltimore. Since you weren't
around, I guess I had more time to gossip and to fritter
away the days. Anyway, she had the whole village in a
great commotion most of the time. In the first place,
she didn't think any of us worthy of her. She was a
cousin to Lady Somebody-or-other — Lady Shaw, that
was it — and she gave herself such airs! She had with
her a servant from London, but could keep no others.
I think they found her too unbearable to work for.
They would go and live there for a few days and then
leave. She was a dreadful woman. Even Father could
not abide her, and you know he can find good in everyone."

"But about Plantation House?" Edward prodded.

"Oh, yes. Lady Shaw, the cousin, you know, had lived
in India. Her husband, who must have been Lord Shaw,

I suppose, was somehow connected with the East India Company. After they came back to England, they built a place in the country not far from London, and furnished it with what must have been a whole boatload of outlandish furniture and things from India. They called it Plantation House. You would think they would give it an Indian name, wouldn't you? So Mrs. — oh, dear, what was the dreadful woman's name? Anyway, she was forever saying in a loud, braying voice, 'When I visit with Lady Shaw at Plantation House, I have several servants to wait upon me.' It became a sort of byword in the village, you may be sure. And ever since, whenever any of us wished to put on airs, we would say, 'When I sup at Plantation House' or 'At Plantation House we never do this or that!' So it was perfectly natural that Amelia should assign Plantation House to us as our new home."

He laughed. Then, stretching himself slowly like a cat, he got to his feet.

"This palace of planks is your Tent, and not our Plantation House, Eliza. But I will build you one, and I think I know exactly where. Come, do you feel like a little walk? I can put off my tentmaking for another hour or so."

He stretched out his hand, and she stood beside him. That particular tone of Edward's voice was always reserved for moments of importance.

"Wait until I put this in a safe place," she said. "You have several shirts, and it would be no great tragedy if something should happen to this one. But needles are precious here, and I have only two or three, I think, so

I must take care of them. Although," she added, after she had rolled up the shirt with the needle carefully fastened inside and tucked it into a crotch in a nearby tree, "I'm sure if I should lose all of them, you would find a way to make one for me."

"You give me credit for talents I don't possess, I fear," he murmured, but she noticed that he looked pleased.

They walked past their cave and on through the brush, which was not thick enough to require cutting.

"See the palm trees?" he said, holding back a vine so that she could pass without catching her turban. "I spotted them from the spring. And there are coconuts on them. That means good food for us, a welcome change from our usual fare, and delicious coconut milk to drink. Ah, I was right. There, Liza, that's what I wanted you to see."

He stopped and pulled her close to him. She stared ahead and saw the most enormous tree she had ever seen in her life. Its trunk was gnarled and buttressed, and seemed to be made of many trunks, all twisted and grown together, and its branches covered an area as large as her father's entire property back in Awbury, she thought. Over it all was a sort of golden shine that came, she supposed, from some trick of tropical sunlight on glistening leaf.

"Edward, what is it?" she exclaimed. "It's so enormous! I thought the elms at home were large. This is bigger than any of them."

He beamed on the tree with the great pride of one who has created something, not merely discovered it.

"A silk-cotton tree," he told her. "Mr. Dickinson showed me one on his property, and said that they grew to a very great size, although his was not nearly as large as this one. They always stand alone, he told me, never in groups or groves like most trees."

"A whole grove of these trees would be beyond belief," she murmured. "Even one is — almost frightening."

They were silent for a moment, staring at the tree. "In time," he said, "the leaves will fall off, and blossoms shaped like bells take their place, and later there are pods that are odd in some way." Then he led her under its wide branches and beyond, so that they stood on clear ground, with the huge tree just behind them.

"There is our Lake, Eliza. It is even more alluring from here, isn't it, so calm and with the trees clustered on its rim, and the rocky point stretching out into it. How dark the rocks are — Black Point we should call it, I think. Isn't this a beautiful spot, Eliza? Here I will build you your Plantation House."

She slipped her hand in his, thinking that if the occasion arose, he could and would build her a fine house.

"There could be no better situation for it," she agreed.

"But first I'll work on the palace we've already begun, before we start worrying about a larger one! Oh, Eliza, look!" he exclaimed.

Her eyes followed the direction of his pointing finger, and she saw the silver shapes of fish shooting up from the water near the rocky point. They leaped high in the air, then splashed back into the sea again in a way that seemed pointless to her.

"What are they? Why do they jump so?"

"They're mullet. We ate them at the Dickinsons', if you remember, and you liked them particularly."

"Why don't we bring over the lines and try to catch them?"

"A funny thing about them, they can't be caught on ordinary bait. They won't take it. They jump toward the light for reasons of their own. I hadn't known they would leap like that during the day, but thought it only at twilight. However, there they are. Perhaps there is something peculiar about the light at this moment. Mr. Dickinson told me how the natives catch them, and we'll try it some evening. When we've nothing else to do," he added with a wry smile.

They left the leaping fish and returned slowly to the Tent, as Edward pointed out trees that he called Indian fig trees, aloes, cabbage palm.

"How do you know what they are?" she asked petulantly. "You have never been on this island before or even on one like it. Or have you been deceiving me all this time?"

"Mr. Dickinson pointed them out to me in Jamaica. I thank Mr. Dickinson daily," he added soberly. "He thought that we would find much the same conditions in St. George's Cay as obtained on his island, and he attempted to teach me much."

"And did," Eliza said.

"Apparently more of it penetrated my head than I was aware of," Edward told her. "I just hope I don't get things mixed up, and insist that some poisonous plant is edible."

"I don't worry about that," she told him confidently.

"I don't worry about anything you do — except your overdoing, perhaps."

When they got back to the Ridge, she settled down with her sewing and he worked for a while at the plank house. Then he decided he had had enough for the day.

"I think we should come here first thing in the morning, and work until the sun gets too high for comfort," he decided. "Let's go back, Eliza."

She found it hot walking in the sun, but realized that he, who had been working so hard, must be even warmer.

"Oh, dear, if only there were no sharks," she said, "we could bathe in that water. Think how cool and refreshing it would be."

Edward mopped his brow. "I thought the sharks would forget about us in time," he admitted, "but they seem to be hoping for more charity. However, as soon as the Tent is done, I'll see if I can't push some boards or branches into the sand to make a sort of stockade, enclosing a space large enough so that we can at least cool off, if not swim, as we've promised ourselves we would learn to do."

Eliza had promised herself no such thing, but she let the moment go by without comment.

"You have enough to worry about," she said shortly. "But it would be wonderful to have a sort of little bathing place of our own sometime."

The next morning early, Eliza watched her husband shoulder another load of planks and carry them up to the Ridge. Since she could see him at his work up there, she stayed on board and determined to get all the rest of the fruits and vegetables up from the hold. Shaddocks, oranges, and limes were spread out evenly on deck when Edward came back from his work on the Ridge.

"Everything is fine," she said, "except for that one pineapple. I'm afraid it's too ripe, although I think part of it is still fit to eat."

"At home the rich people eat these for dessert," Edward told her, "But we are richer than they, because we can afford to have pineapple for breakfast."

He took it from her, and she watched with interest as he twisted the top of it gently but firmly, until he had pulled out a deep cone of fibers.

"I'll plant this," he said. "That's how they told me to do in Jamaica — twist out the top. We can put it in the sandy place near the melons. And now, Mrs. Seaward, may I tempt you?"

Later that day they came upon another delicacy. This time it was a huge turtle that they surprised on the sand, where she had scooped a nest with one of her forefins and had laid some eggs in the depression. For the first time since they had found themselves on the island, the Seawards came perilously close to quarreling. Edward caught and tied up the turtle, then went back to the ship for a knife. Eliza, biting her lip, said firmly that there was no need to kill the creature and that he was turning himself into a murderer.

"We don't need the fresh meat, Ned," she cried. "Fidele keeps us supplied with iguanas, heaven knows, and the meat would be about the same to taste, wouldn't it? And that poor animal — what is to be gained by just willfully slaughtering it."

"Fresh meat is fresh meat," he insisted stubbornly. "You don't suppose our friends the sharks out there would let us go free if they happened to have had a good meal recently?"

Eliza fled to the deck of the ship and put herself as far from Edward and the turtle as possible. There was something about the helplessness of the creature, lying on its back and waving its feet in the air, that upset her. She tried to tell herself that Edward was always right in these matters, but she still couldn't bring herself around to his way of thinking.

"Liza?" she heard him call, as he made his way up the ladder. Reluctantly she left the shelter of the deck house and walked toward him. He held his shirt up so that there was a pocket of the material, and she could see that he held something there with gingerly care.

"You were right, Eliza," he said at once, with a sheepish smile. "I found I could no more kill that creature than I could have plunged a knife into Fidele! To kill something tied hand and foot is a little more than I could ever manage, I feel sure. But here are some of her eggs; the rest were smashed when I captured the lady, I'm afraid. There are only four of them."

Eliza looked at him with delight.

"I'm so glad," she murmured. "Really, Edward, you have no idea. And thank you for the eggs. There's flour below, and I just found a little cask of raisins. I'll make you a proper English pudding, and you won't miss your turtle steak one whit, I promise you."

She took the eggs, looking curiously at the skin that covered them.

"Aren't they odd?" she marveled. "Somehow they look to be all yolk, don't they? Edward, look up there." She gestured with her head, her hands being occupied with the turtle eggs, and he turned to see what it was that she wanted to show him.

"See the sun catch our new palace!" she exclaimed. "Doesn't it look sturdy and secure up there, even though it's not finished? Look, Ned, at your Eliza's tent! A piece of canvas for shade, that was all that I asked of you. And what do I get? A palace, made of planks!"

CHAPTER 6

A Time to Talk

WHEN THEY HAD BEEN on the island a little more than two weeks, Eliza found that they had settled into a comfortable routine that made their lives there seem matter-of-fact as well as peaceful. The foods that she cooked were not those she had helped prepare in Awbury, nor did she have a kitchen, with hearth and an iron kettle on a crane and an oven in the chimney bricks. Instead of peas and beans from the rectory garden, she had fingerlike plantains to boil or bake, as well as coccos and pumpkins. There were melons, oranges, and pineapples to eat raw, and big pear-shaped shaddock. Familiar fish were never to be found in the warm waters around them, but sometimes Edward managed to hook or spear some large creature that had pursued smaller fish into the shallows, and of course every so often Fidele obliged them by catching and killing an iguana. The open fire on the sand by the bow of the boat seemed no longer so difficult to her, and she had quite an array of utensils from the ship's galley. The galley itself they had agreed never to use, because of the danger of setting fire to the ship. Edward kept a supply of wood handy on the beach, and since they had found the tinderbox, she was able to light the fire herself, and could now prepare a meal without his help.

One problem that had arisen had almost caused friction between them — that of laundry. Eliza, one morning, gathered together a bundle of clothes which she proposed to take to wash in the water running below the spring.

"You are not a washerwoman, Mrs. Seaward," Edward had reminded her.

"I am the likeliest candidate I can see," she replied teasingly.

"You have never had to wash clothes," he said sharply. "And I do not intend that you should begin now."

"I have never eaten lizards, nor cooked in a ring of rocks on the sand, nor lived aboard a beached brig," she said with asperity. "But the experience hasn't hurt me. The minister's daughters were brought up without servants, you know. The rectory was not Lady Shaw's Plantation House."

"You always had someone in to launder for you, I know that," he said hotly. "I will wash these things, Eliza."

"You were never brought up to wash clothes either," she said. "Oh, Edward, what are we quarreling about?"

He grinned at her sheepishly. "Sometimes I despair," he said finally. "at what I have brought you to. And I promised you so much — a fine house, servants — "

"I invited myself on this voyage," she reminded him. "I haven't complained, have I?"

"Indeed you haven't." He swept her into his arms and held her tightly for a moment. "And I don't know why I should snap at you like a turtle. Tell you what, Liza, we will both do the laundry, and we will have two stout helpers. Wait and see."

The "helpers" turned out to be two sturdy paddles that he had made, and he showed her how to pound the clothes on a smooth stone in the little river. Then he helped her spread them to dry and bleach in the sun.

"Now how could you know about *that?*" she demanded, eyeing her paddle and the whiteness of the clothes with amazement.

"I've heard somewhere that people in hot countries wash their clothes this way," he said.

"From Mr. Dickinson, no doubt?"

"No," he laughed. "Not from Mr. Dickinson this time. We did not discuss laundry, of that I'm sure."

So to the chores of cooking, cleaning, and sewing, Eliza added a once-a-week session with the laundry paddles in the stream. Feeding the poultry was, of course, a daily affair. The hens and goats foraged for themselves, but were given additional food by Eliza, in the form of spoiled or spoiling fruit and vegetables, and occasional pieces of iguana or fish, because they remembered that even the hens needed some animal foods occasionally. The ducks had, by this time, been added to the others in the cavern and they lived there peacefully enough, waddling to the brook whenever they liked, and showing no inclination to leave their new quarters.

"How beautiful it is," Eliza remarked one evening as they watched the sun go down beyond the high ridge of the island to the west. "And how idyllic to live in a place where it is always warm and pleasant."

"Always?" Edward raised an eyebrow and looked at her quizzically. "Have you forgotten the circumstances of our arrival?"

Eliza giggled. "Hardly," she said. "But it has been fine for so long. Perhaps that was a freak storm of some kind."

Later, she said it was a judgment on her optimism, because the very next day there was almost no sea breeze to cool them off in the delightful way they were used to, and that evening the western horizon was dark and overcast. Edward and Eliza went up to their plank house on the Ridge, where they thought they might catch whatever breeze there was, and were amusing themselves by feeding melon rinds to the goats. Suddenly the sky blackened noticeably and the goats just as suddenly deserted them, running back to the comfort and security of their cave.

"They know more than we do," Edward remarked grimly. "Come, let's go back to the ship, Eliza. By the look of it, it will begin to rain before long."

They hadn't gone more than ten yards toward the *Mary* when the heavens seemed to open up and poured rain down on them in great torrents. Hand in hand and laughing, they ran back to the ship as fast as they could, but were drenched to the skin, their hair and clothes plastered to their bodies, and Fidele, hard at their heels, looked more like a drowned rat than a dog.

At first Eliza, as they changed into the dry clothes, tried to think of it as a lark, but she was upset in spite of herself.

"Why is it so calm and quiet?" she asked. "It seems so — ominous. Why is there no wind?"

"Would you like there to be wind? I seem to remember you didn't care much for it when it blew so violently the day we came here."

"It doesn't seem right, somehow. Oh, I know what it is. You told me then that a dead calm precedes a hurricane. Oh, Edward, are we to have another of those awful hurricanes? I'm — I'm frightened."

"There is nothing to be afraid of, not this time, Liza," he told her soothingly. "We are on dry land now, you know. Well, perhaps not exactly dry land, but we are not afloat. Our ship is stuck fast in the sand, and is firmly tied to rocks on both sides."

She was comforted by this, but when, later, the wind came up and blew fully as violently as she had remembered, she saw that her husband's face was drawn and grim. He went frequently to the companionway door and looked out, returning with his face and head streaming with water.

"It is all right, Eliza. The ropes will hold. They are stronger than they look," he reported, telling her without realizing it exactly what it was that worried him.

They remained below until dawn, when the wind began to die away and the rain stopped, so that they could open up the cabin windows to let things dry out. Edward mopped up the water in the companionway and on the cabin floor, and Eliza got their wet clothes ready to take up to the deck to dry out when the sun appeared again, but she had been awake too long and before Edward returned from his swabbing she had gone to sleep. When at last she woke up, she was indignant to hear that Edward had been ashore to inspect the livestock, which he pronounced perfectly safe inside the cave, and to see what damage had been done to the Tent. He was pleased to report that it had lost only two planks from the roof, both of which had fallen nearby and were easily replaced.

"The weather isn't going to be — what did you call it, idyllic? — for a spell yet," he said. "I think we might as well resign ourselves to a day or two perhaps of living on board. Maybe more."

They found that they missed their pleasant chores ashore, and since neither of them was content to sit in idleness, Edward decided to make a small table for the Tent, and Eliza began to sew on two new pairs of gaiters for them, since it was evident that their first ones wouldn't last forever. As they worked, they talked and planned; at first, for the most part, about where they would plant the fruit seeds, the yams, and the coccos, and where they should sow the Indian corn they had brought from Jamaica. Eliza reflected that, except for their bizarre surroundings, they might be any farm couple planning for the future.

During the rainy days, the water seemed to blow across the island in great sheets and vanish over the sea, and while they were forced to remain on the *Mary*, finding numerous little tasks to keep their hands busy, they found more and more time to talk. Together all of the time, as they had been, when the weather was fair they were too busy to talk as they worked, and too tired to converse at any length when they stopped. On fine days they rose early, worked for the long morning hours, ate dinner, and then took an ever-lengthening siesta, each dropping into a profound sleep. After that, they worked again for a while, ate a simple evening meal in the Tent, and were on the *Mary* in bed and asleep almost before the sky had finished darkening each evening. But now they were cooped up together, and for hours on end found their tongues wagging endlessly.

At first their talk turned to Awbury, quite naturally, since their thoughts were so much there, but after a while, Eliza began to notice that the locale had quickly shifted from Awbury to Bristol. Edward did that purposely, she realized, and thanked him for it. Bristol was — safe. It did not teem with memories and edge on tears. Bristol was home, but it was also part of their great adventure.

Edward, of course, knew Bristol much better than she did, and she encouraged him to talk about it to her, reminding her of things she had perhaps only glimpsed and now scarcely remembered. He liked to speak of the old Christmas Steps, where he often visited bookshops and dealers in curios; of the ancient gateway, one of the original four, where were the carved figures, painted red and blue, of Bryn and Belinus, who were supposed to have founded the city nearly six centuries before; of the huge Town Chest in the Town Hall, a chest with triple locks so that three keys, held by three different individuals, were required to unlock it.

Eliza's most vivid picture of Bristol was the one that was engraved on her mind, the long last look at it as it receded into the past over the *Mary*'s stern. She could

see the eminence of Brandon Hill, which Edward told
her had been given by Queen Elizabeth to the spinsters
of Bristol so that they could hang out their washing
there, and the many spires, each uniquely shaped,
which Edward seemed to enjoy describing and identify-
ing for her. St. Mary Redcliffe, which Queen Bess herself had pronounced "the fairest, goodliest and most
famous parish church in England"; the English Renais-
sance tower of St. Stephen's; the church of St. John,
built on the old city wall. There was All Saints' Church
— "We'll go there one day to see the effigy of Bristol's
benefactor, Edward Colston," he promised her. "And
not far from it the Llandoger Trow Inn, which was
once the haunt of pirates and privateers and slavers — I
used to look at those blackened timbers and fancy I
could see the pirates' swarthy faces," he confessed sheepishly, his eyes gazing wistfully out to sea. "And dream
of finding pirate gold."

Then they were, once more, back on the island and
their immediate life, because the men who had visited
the Llandoger Trow Inn, which was perhaps as much
as two hundred years old, might have sailed these very
waters.

Eliza found the opportunity to ask the questions that
persisted in rising in her mind, while Edward, who had
been thinking too, seemed to dredge up from the great
depths of his retentive and ever-active mind many of
the answers she was seeking.

She was still, quite naturally, most concerned with
where they were in the world, and with their chances
of seeing other people, either those who lived here or

who were, like themselves, castaways, forced off their prescribed routes. Edward, it appeared, had become more and more interested in who their predecessors in the area might have been, and he delved back into his memory for bits of history which he tried to piece together.

"There were, first of all, pirates," he told Eliza thoughtfully, "and if anyone ever visited our island, I think it would be one of those. Until perhaps fifty years ago, most ships moved in fleets. After the ships of discovery and of colonization, there were those which carried the gold and silver and pearls back to the Spanish Crown. The ships that traveled singly, and by stealth, were the pirates. I can't see whole fleets putting into these small islands. For one thing, the coral reefs act as deterrents, as we all too well know. A crafty pirate might find his way through the barrier, for reasons of his own, but the fleets were always in a hurry to get where they were going, and visited only the known ports. If all the tales are true, the Gulf of Mexico was crowded with the scoundrels once," he grinned. "Mr. Dickinson says — "

He grinned again cheerfully and Eliza smiled too. It seemed to them that half of their sentences were prefaced with "Mr. Dickinson says" or "At the Dickinsons' we saw."

"I remember that evening when all the talk was of pirates," Eliza said. "At the time it made no particular impression on me — it was like having someone talk about the men who marched on the Crusades, it seemed so remote. And yet, here we are, in the very ocean

where they sailed and raided. It doesn't sound so colorful, when you find yourself right on the history page,
does it, Ned?"

"That's what it is, though, Liza, just history. There's
nary a pirate alive now, I promise you. And of course
they were colorful, bad a lot as they were. There was
one unprincipled scoundrel, the worst of them all,
according to reports. Well, you know about Morgan —
because of hearing Mr. Dickinson talk about him — and
all the evil things he did. Henry Morgan crisscrossed the
Gulf of Mexico a good many times in his life of crime
and cruelty, and I've no doubt that if ships could leave
tracks behind them as wagons do, we'd have seen his
mark many times."

"He might," Eliza said with a shudder, "have seen
this very island, mightn't he, Ned?"

"He could have been on it," Edward agreed cheerfully. "I told you the pirates put into handy ports, to
hide, or to get water and food, or to careen their ships
so they could repair them. They wouldn't stay, of course.
Pirates were not settlers by nature, and they liked life
afloat far too well."

"How did Morgan happen to live in Jamaica?" Eliza
asked idly. "Was he born there?"

Edward shook his head, then sat back and critically
surveyed the net he was mending, having abandoned
his table temporarily. "I haven't got the hang of it yet,
but it will serve," he said, starting to work on a second
great rent in his net. "Morgan was born near a hundred
years ago. He was Welsh, as I remember it. I don't know
how or why he got to Jamaica. Once there, any man

with his nature, though, would be quick to see this sea as his proper place in the world. The Spanish were taking gold from the Spanish Main and sailing it in their fleets back to Spain once or twice a year. Vera Cruz in Mexico, Porto Bello on the Isthmus, and Cartagena on the Main were the important ports, and they traveled regular trade routes which soon enough became known to the likes of Morgan. Pirates could lurk behind any handy island — this one, perhaps — and wait until the right moment to attack."

"Why didn't the Spanish *do* something about them?"

"They did what they could. Gold was demanded by the King — in fact, gold was the only reason for Spanish interest in the islands and the Main, once its presence was discovered and the quest for the spices of the East abandoned. The fleets were forced to sail with all the gold and silver brought overland, and sail they did. They tried to protect themselves as well as they could.

"For that matter, they feared the English too, you know, because we were forever waging war with the Spaniards, and their plate ships were fair game. Many a Spanish ship lies at the bottom of the sea, unfortunately without a buoy to tell us where. They must have been something to see, Eliza, those Spanish galleons. I've heard the mast was as tall as the ship was long, and the stern stood high and proud."

He spoke so wistfully that Eliza bent over her sewing with a hidden smile. More than once she had heard her father say, "To every man, the age past is more exciting than his own, no matter when he lives," and she knew that for the moment Edward was wishing himself back in the days when the Spanish treasure ships sailed the waters, there for the taking, if a man were brave and lucky enough.

"And the gold lies at the bottom of the sea?" she prompted.

He nodded. "Gold is heavy, and makes excellent ballast for a ship with holes caused by big guns in its hull. But of course much of it was taken off the galleons, or the Spanish ships were seized and sailed to port to be unloaded. The pirates didn't always merely wait for ships either. Morgan attacked Panama and sacked the city, carrying away with him an unbelievable fortune — a million pounds, maybe, in gold and jewels. And still didn't get it all, they say."

"Oh, Edward!" Eliza breathed, trying to imagine even a thousand pounds in gold, and failing. "What happened to all that gold finally?"

"The pirates divided up their loot — and trust that rascal Morgan to cheat his own men, for that's what he did, giving them mere token payments and seizing the rest for himself. The big ones, like Morgan himself, often hid enormous amounts of it. On islands, probably, where it could be recovered when the smoke had cleared up, and suspicious eyes were turned away at last."

"And the wrecks?"

He dropped the net he was working on and flexed his tired fingers, yawning widely.

"I've had enough of *that* work," he announced. "I'll go back to my table for a while. Well, people are always finding old maps and hearing tales from old sailors —

I've heard plenty of that kind of talk right in Bristol. All about treasures here or there, enough to make a man dream his way to riches," he told her. "But a few fathoms of water is as good a barricade as any. Sometimes, of course, it happens that the ships have been sunk in shallow water, where they had steered, hoping to make land, perhaps, and Indians with good lungs and hard masters can dive deep and recover some of the loot. For fifty years or so, people have been experimenting with a diving bell, too, so that divers don't need to surface every time they feel the need for some air. Any way you look at it, though, it's an uneasy business."

"It would be such fun," she said, and this time it was her own voice that had the wistful note, "to find a wreck offshore here, with gold pieces spilling out of it."

"It would be hard work, not fun," he assured her. "And you can't even swim, Mrs. Seaward, for all I made our little bathing place, much less become a diver. Oh, Liza, I didn't mean to tease you. It would be fun, of course. And who knows, on one of our excursions in the boat I'm going to make, we may find ourselves looking down through the water at the rotting hull of a Spanish ship, with its specially built rooms full of gold and silver ingots and coins, waiting for us to find them!"

Suddenly, with both hands, he grasped a stick lying at his feet and broke it sharply against his knee with a motion of violence rare to him.

"It would be fun *and* hard work," he said darkly, "but more than that, it would be profitable. We have been less than three weeks on this miserable island. So much time we can afford. But suppose it becomes six weeks — three months — six months — even more? For that time we have nothing to show but our lives, with perhaps our ribs showing through our skin, and scratches and calluses on our hands. Is this the way I promised to provide for you? Must we go on forever, living like Adam and Eve and scratching our very food out of the ground? I tell you —" He stood up angrily, looked off toward the land, and said abruptly, "The rain has stopped at last. I'll fetch the water," and was gone before she could so much as gasp at him. She had not known how inadequate he held himself, or how strongly he felt that life was passing them by.

CHAPTER 7

A Cup of Chocolate

EDWARD'S BLACK mood was only temporary. Nothing was said about it later by either of them, but when Edward returned with his cask of fresh water he brought with him a coconut, a still-wiggling fish which he had managed to catch, and a beautiful polished shell for Eliza's collection. The treasures represented, she understood, an apology, and the moment was ostensibly forgotten. Soon the weather cleared too, so they took a walk ashore, pleased to find things very little disturbed. Much seaweed had been tossed up on the beach, and many shells, but they decided not to explore at this time. They would go only to look at the Tent, at their garden, and at the cave. At each place they found everything to be in good order.

When they returned to the *Mary* with a fresh supply of water from the spring, Eliza set the table for tea, using Edward's new table, and was happy to see how much her simple action pleased him.

"Thank you for the compliment, Liza," he said fondly. "It isn't much of a table, to be sure, but it's a miracle to me that it looks as much like a table as it does! We have so many talents we didn't even suspect in ourselves, don't we?"

"You do," Eliza said shortly, wondering when, if ever, she would have a chance to prove herself equal to their odd life.

The next day was Sunday, so, according to their custom, they put aside their work and went for a walk, this time exploring the beach and looking at the strange objects that had been cast up by the storm. It was Fidele, as usual, who discovered a huge crayfish in the act of trying to eat a fish that had been stranded. Edward somewhat gingerly thrust a pike into the creature's large, formidable curved claw, and the crayfish seized the iron point of the pike with such strength that Edward was able to drag it along the beach. Fidele apparently thought he would like to attack his strange adversary again, but Eliza, taking one shuddering look at its spiny shell and the two great claws, snatched the dog to her, while Edward managed to tie the stranger's claws.

"This will give us a meal fit for kings," he told her. "I've been told that these crayfish — I think, because of those claws, this might be actually called a lobster — are fine eating."

"Mr. Dickinson, no doubt?" Eliza teased, and he nodded.

"Mr. Dickinson, that fount of all information! Did you ever stop to think, Eliza, what would have happened if we hadn't stopped in Jamaica and learned all we did from Mr. Dickinson?"

A day later, after they had eaten it, Edward began to

wonder if perhaps Mr. Dickinson had omitted something they needed to know about the crayfish. They had boiled the creature in their largest pot, cracked its shell, and eaten it while it was still hot. The taste, new to them, they found to be pleasant enough, although a little stronger than they would have liked, which they thought perhaps was due to its great size. The next day they went to work in their garden, planting melon and pumpkin, and the seeds of oranges and limes that they had saved. In the heat of the day they stopped working and sat in the shade of the silk-cotton tree, eating the meat of the crayfish which they had taken with them, sprinkling it with lime juice and some ground capsicums.

"This tree," Edward said dreamily, looked up at its tremendous ceiling over their heads, "seems to mean something to me. It is so large that it might be a landmark. In other words, if a ship should sail near this coast, it would surely notice this tree immediately. Perhaps that is why it seems so important to me."

"We didn't even see it," Eliza pointed out. "We'd been here at least a week, maybe longer, before we saw it. *You* saw it," she amended.

"We approached the island through a back door, as it were," he told her. "The double ring of reefs around Seaward's Island protects it from people like us, but our storm somehow got us over and through them both. More properly, a ship would come here from the west, and even then it needs to know the breaks in the reef and the channels of the lagoons. But you see, a ship coming from the northeast or northwest would see first of all our Hill, and then, closer in, our Tree, our silk-cotton tree. It means something," he finished stubbornly. "Something to me, at any rate."

"Perhaps," Eliza said, taking his knife from him and cutting into an orange which she then handed to him to eat, "it is because someday we are going to build a house here, near the Tree. Perhaps that is why it seems to mean something to you."

"Maybe." He shrugged. She wondered at his apparent indolence, after he had finished his orange. He usually seemed impatient to be up and about, after his noonday meal. Today, however, he appeared to be willing to dawdle. He took the seeds from their oranges, planted them carefully in the northeast corner of the open space where they were, and, to her surprise, sat down again.

"One day we'll have an orange grove there," he said, looking about him idly, and showing no inclination to get back to work. When at last he returned to his planting, she watched him with growing apprehension. Before long she knew why he moved so slowly and disinterestedly today. Her dinner seemed to weigh heavily and uneasily in her, and she realized that Edward was suffering from the same trouble. Once, when he returned to her, he saw by her face that she felt ill, and he said, "So, it is not just I, Eliza. I'm afraid it must be our friend the crayfish. There must be something about it that we don't know, that Mr. Dickinson should have told us. Perhaps we shouldn't have kept it for a second day. That is more than possible. Well, we have learned something, at least. Do you feel too badly? No — you're sure? Let's go sit in the Tent for a bit and then go back to our cabin. I don't feel up to doing a day's work at the moment, and I doubt if you do either."

With the rains, as well as the crayfish and its resultant discomfort, behind them, they settled again into their placid routine. The days, now that it was the middle of January, were growing longer, although it was a good four months to mid-May, when the days would be fourteen hours and more in length, and hot. Edward had devised a schedule for them that would enable him to get the greater part of the work over with before those long days of intense heat should arrive, and that would allow him to take advantage of the shade as much as possible. The plantation, which was the way they thought of their special clearing by the silk-cotton tree, was in the shade for nearly four hours after sunrise, and the sun came up at seven. From midmorning until close to the sunset hour, the Tent was in shade, and the pathway between the Tent and the *Mary* was in the shadow of the Hill for the first hours of the day. These periods of grateful shade would be shortened, though, as the year wore along, and Edward insisted that the work be done well in advance of that time.

Still, with the Tent finished and with so many seeds planted, the great sense of urgency had left them, and Eliza had pointed out that they were both growing thinner, although they were eating well, and that they, Edward especially, were overtired much of the time and should ease up on their labors. The garden had not yet reached the point of requiring much attention, and the livestock took care of itself, quite contentedly foraging in the underbrush and roaming between the cave, the spring, and the plank house. The goat that had broken its leg seemed to be getting along so well that Edward took off its splints, remarking that Limpy was surely going to have her kid soon as would Mab, and that the size of the island's population would be increased.

With a newly relaxed schedule, they found that they had more time to explore and to enjoy what they found. They saw tiny birds, on wings that whirred so rapidly they could scarcely be seen, feeding from the brilliant flowers. Some notes that reminded them of the nightingales at home drew them into the forest, to look in vain for the songsters, and the cooing of doves around their silk-cotton tree delighted them. The noise of parrakeets, far less musical, lured Eliza to the summit of the hill near the clearing and she saw them there in their green feathers, picking industriously at the fruit clustered in the tops of the palm trees. She even ventured, once or twice, to go down alone to the edge of the Lake. There she saw fish swimming in the placid, clear water, and gulls, cormorants, and diving waterfowl hunting for food or sitting quietly in the sun. Every day brought out some new wonder, and there was still the whole island to be explored. Edward was particularly anxious to walk around their Lake, so that they could discover whether it was a subterranean channel or an opening to the sea that made it salt.

It was not all perfect, by any means. Sometimes sandflies suddenly appeared from nowhere and swarmed and bit savagely, driving them to the *Mary*, where they fretted inside their wooden jail. Occasionally, when the breeze died away, they suffered an almost unbearable heat from which there was no escape but to bathe inside the stockade in shallow water that had become warm and sticky. Several times Edward came back from his gardens, his face dark with anger because a vine had withered or a blight had spoiled an immature fruit tree, and then Eliza held her tongue, knowing it would be useless to remind him that the trees and vines and plants grew rapidly and bore prodigiously, knowing, too, the black mood would pass.

Once in a while, the incessant rustling of the palm trees seemed deafening, and Eliza felt as though she must scream at them to be quiet. Most of all, she hated the too-frequent days when a lethargy came over them both, when moving was an effort, and only the most essential chores could be attempted.

"Tropical torpor," Edward called it, with a grin that in itself seemed to cost him effort. "And we must watch ourselves, because it can surely spread from body to mind. Once we feel that nothing is worth doing, we are lost, Eliza."

But the rest of the time, the cord of their life spun on smoothly, with small moments of discovery and achievement strung on its length like pearls. Sometimes Edward cut down a coconut tree, and they ate the unusual meat of the nuts and drank the delicious milk. Near the silk-cotton tree there were Indian figs — prickly pears Mr. Dickinson had called them in Jamaica — and Edward knew that they were good to eat, but the spines or thorns on their sides had so far discouraged him from making the attempt. He was forever on the lookout, though, for new foods, aware that the stores aboard the *Mary* would not last indefinitely and wanting as much variety in their diet as possible. They were both particularly concerned with tea. There was a good supply of it on the ship, as well as plenty of sugar and enough coffee to last them for some time, but without saying the words out loud, the Seawards had come to a mutual recognition of the fact that they might be on the island for the rest of their lives. It was more than possible, even though it didn't bear discussing, at least not yet.

Edward's eyes, constantly searching for new sources of food, found some trees one day that had not been noticed before. Edward and Eliza were paying a visit to the cave, and by now the thicket had become so familiar to them that they seldom looked about, but made for the cavern and their livestock almost automatically.

"Look, Liza, there among the acacias," he said, stopping suddenly in the path, so that Eliza almost bumped into him. "Oh, sorry. Those trees with the pods on them — they look like cucumbers, only brown? And see, some of them have burst open. Let's go find out what was in them." He dove into the thicket, calling back, "Better wait there. No sense scratching yourself all up just to satisfy my curiosity. Ah, here they are. Seeds of some kind, I would say. Look, I'll bring them out to you."

He held some of the seeds in the palm of his hand, and promptly put one into his mouth, biting down on it.

"Edward Seaward, someday you will chew a deadly poison," she scolded. "You said yourself you might, you know."

"I'm not swallowing it," he said patiently. "Say, Liza, you know what this is? Here, try one. It's chocolate! No, really, try it. I've seen chocolate nuts — cacao, they're called — at home, only much larger than this. Probably these, because they haven't been cultivated but grow in their wild state, are smaller than those in Jamaica or those carried back home. Well, Liza, that may solve a problem for us. It will be a long time before our tea gives out, but now, at least, we know we can make ourselves a substitute drink, which will extend the supply even farther. Why, yes, don't look so surprised, you know that the Spaniards drink chocolate and think very highly of it, and I understand that at home some of the wealthy people like to affect it for breakfast, or instead of tea at teatime. We shall be nothing if not fashionable, Eliza. These nuts should be pounded into powder, then boiled with milk and water and sugar. I believe we will find it to be a treat indeed. Let's gather as many as we can, and experiment with them back at our ship. And I will spread some of that rich, black dirt I found at the back of the cave along the roots of these trees. Perhaps we can have larger chocolate nuts in time."

Eliza wanted to moan, "Oh, Edward, more work! And just so that you can give me a cup of chocolate!" But she had learned to bite back her words of protest. They had no effect on him, she knew, and served only to displease him.

"I'll finish my cleaning," she told him, proud that she could let him go to the cave without having her watch him. The Tent had given her a great sense of freedom. She knew she could see him at work wherever he was, except when he disappeared briefly behind some trees or in the Cave, but she no longer felt the need to keep her eyes constantly on him. Now she turned to their plank house, which by this time Edward had fitted with a bed and shelves, easily made by pushing boards through the chinks in the walls. The bed had at first been intended as a settee of sorts, for their use during the daytime, but lately they had begun to think of sleeping on shore, especially on the warmer nights, and Eliza had several armloads of linen and blankets to dispose on the shelves so that they would be ready for use at any time. She had already arranged her growing collection of shells on a low shelf, where they would show to best advantage. She found that she was constantly drawn to this array of treasures, and that she liked to pause once in a while in her work to finger the cool, smooth surfaces and to delight in the strange shapes and soft, subtle colors.

Edward was away longer than she had expected. She had glanced out several times and had seen him moving between the cave and the chocolate trees. When she finished her work, she sat down on a seat he had made, in front of the house, to wait for him. It was quiet, except for the occasional cry of a bird and the perpetual soft rustle of the palm leaves. On her right, she could see the blue waters of the sea, with the line of treacherous reefs piercing the surface, each rock surrounded by white foam as the breakers broke on their sides. Within the reef barrier, the lagoon was calm and the blue tinged with green. Below, where she could not see it from her perch, the placid waters of the lake or harbor would lie blue and sparkling. Ahead to the north, on her left, her eyes gazed on high, jagged rocks and the wooded peaks of the island, its folds covered with the jungle greens that had once seemed mysterious and even ominous and now were merely pleasant to the eye. With Edward, who must be in the cave, out of sight, she found herself completely alone in the world, a tiny figure surrounded by a universe that stretched endlessly away.

Restless, Eliza wished that Edward would come back. Edward had become her world, if indeed he hadn't always been, she thought, and even a few moments' absence from him was hard to tolerate.

"Wake up, Fidele," she said, gently nudging the sleeping dog with her foot. "Let's go find our lord and master."

At that very instant, however, he appeared at the mouth of the cave, and as he emerged into the sunlight, she saw that he carried something in his hand. At first she thought it might be a snake. She gasped, because they had never seen a snake on the island, and Edward had told her that he felt sure they never would. Then she realized that it did not move, and that he did not appear to clutch it tightly, so it must be some inanimate object. He walked so slowly, however, continuing to stare at it, that she felt some tiny hand of fear touch her heart. For Edward to be surprised . . .

"Eliza," he said, when he was close to her, and she saw that his eyes were grave and that his face was white under his tan. "Eliza, I have — found something odd. Look here."

She took her eyes from his face with difficulty, and looked at the object that he held out to her.

"But —"

"It is a belt," he said. "Or what is left of one. This is leather — you can see where it's rotted through. And this is a buckle of brass, and it seems to have a military design of some sort. See, I scoured it with sand, to get it clearer."

She raised her eyes to his.

"But, Edward," she whispered. "What does it mean?"

"It means," he said, "that someone has been on our island before us. Some years ago, I would say by the condition of the belt, but someone has been here. I found it in the cave, when I was digging just now. If it had been on the beach, or even somewhere near it, I would guess that perhaps it was washed ashore with some wreckage, and had been blown, or moved by some animal, to another spot. But the fact that I discovered it in the cave, and well buried under what I believed to be decayed leaves — I think the meaning of its being there is unmistakable."

He looked at her, and putting the belt on the seat where she had just been, took her hand.

"Don't look so frightened, Liza," he said gently. "There is nothing to be afraid of. It's a surprise, that is all. Whoever owned that belt is no longer here, nor has he been for a great many years, I promise you."

Eliza was ashamed of the panic that seized her, and she determined not to let Edward see it. "Oh, Edward," she said, and was pleased to hear that her voice was in complete control, "you remember how Charlotte has always cautioned you on your tendency to overdo things. Wait until she hears that you went about providing me with a cup of chocolate, and succeeded in uncovering a full-fledged mystery, at the same time."

CHAPTER 8

Life as Usual

THE BELT WAS never far from her mind. Over and over she reminded herself that Edward had said the belt's owner could not be alive on the island today, that if there were other human beings on the island, she and Edward would by this time have known about it.

"They would have seen our smoke, and come to investigate, and we would have seen theirs," he assured her. "We have made no effort to hide ourselves, nor to be quiet, after the first day or two. We have no idea how large this island is, but even though it must be fairly sizable, something would have revealed the presence of others. Forget about the belt, Eliza. It is curious and mysterious and I find it most interesting, but it is not a cause for fear."

After several days, Eliza felt the subject must be pursued, if only to restore her peace of mind. It was not quite enough for her to be told that they were the only inhabitants on the island; she felt she must be sure about it.

"Ned," she began tentatively one day as they were preparing for their midday siesta. "Ned, tell me who

you think might have been on the island. No, don't
look at me like that, I have a right to know. You must
have some theory, and I think I have a right to hear it."

He gave her a long, searching look, and replied, "I
think perhaps you have, Liza. And certainly we'll discuss it, if it will dispel whatever notions you have of
savages and lurking shapes. But you must remember
one thing, Mrs. Seaward. As omniscient as your husband
is, he really doesn't *know* who could have been here.
You will remember that, won't you?"

"Of course, Edward," she said impatiently. "Now
please tell me."

"Ever since we found that soldier's belt," he told her
slowly, "I have been wracking my brain, trying to remember everything I have ever heard about these
islands. And of course right there looms our first big
question, because we don't even know on what island
we're living. However, as I showed you on the captain's
disreputable charts, we can assume we are somewhere
between Jamaica and Honduras, and we have no reason
to believe that we are much to the south of a straight
line drawn between those two places."

Eliza nodded. He had showed her the charts, which
were torn and soiled and had been scribbled over carelessly, arousing Edward to new heights in expressing
his opinion of the general character and slovenly nature
of Captain Molesworth.

"If he were not dead, which he must be, thanks to
his own pigheadedness and stupidity, I would recom-
mend to my uncle that the idiot be discharged at once,"
he had said violently. "If," he added, with a crooked
grin, "I were in a position to say anything to my uncle!"

He sighed, stretched and relaxed again. "Our belt's owner," he went on, "could have been a colonist, or a member of a pirate ship. Probably we will never know which."

He rolled over on his side and looked up at the belt, which he had placed on the edge of a high shelf. "You know, Eliza, I wasn't entirely surprised when I found it."

"You weren't!"

"Well, yes, I was surprised. But at the same time it had crossed my mind, in a vague sort of way, that there could have been someone here once."

"And you didn't tell me," she said reproachfully.

"What could I tell you? It was all so vague in my mind."

"But what made you think of it? Have you seen — other things?"

"Like the belt? No. But — well, the chocolate trees, for one thing. When we saw those that day it popped into my head that someone must have brought them here."

"*Brought* them here? Wouldn't they just grow, like other trees?"

"Probably I remembered wrongly, but it seemed to me that Mr. Dickinson, who certainly did his best to stuff my head full of information, did mention something about the chocolate or cacao trees having been introduced to Jamaica by the Spanish. But then, as I say, he told me so many things, sometimes I believe they're all scrambled up in my head. And yes, to answer your question, they could have just grown here. What I'm trying to say is that, at the moment we first spied the trees, that thought flashed across my mind and was gone. So it served, perhaps, as a sort of preparation for the finding of the belt."

She thought about this for a moment. Then she asked quietly, "Who would the people be who were here, do you think?"

"Shipwrecked people, like ourselves, people blown off their course who also wondered where providence had taken them."

"Or —" she prodded.

"Or — well, at one time there might have been a whole colony here, a town perhaps, or a settlement or two. Although it does seem as though we'd have found something, a blackened stone, a rusted knife blade — something."

"We haven't seen much of the island," she said thoughtfully.

"That, of course, is true. We have worn tracks between the *Mary,* the spring, the cave, the plantation by the tree, and this Tent of ours. We have been too busy to explore further, although one of these days we must. We must make ourselves a boat, for one thing. In it we can move along the shore, which is considerably easier than trying to penetrate the thickets or climb some of these promontories that present their blank faces to us." He yawned and looked narrowly at his wife. "Don't look so despairing, Eliza. I know that imagination of yours, and I can all but see it work on your face. You are thinking we will build a boat and row it around a point of land, straight into the arms of a thriving city almost the size of Bristol and entirely populated with pirates and wild savages!"

"Oh, Edward!" she said, smiling in spite of herself. "But even if we haven't seen much, surely from the Tree, where we have such a fine view, or from here, we would see the remains of a settlement, if there had been one."

"Not necessarily. In this climate, unkind to metal and wood and even to stone, things crumble away rapidly, and the jungle hides the scars. If we didn't keep at our own little garden, I think the wild growth around us would creep back and swallow its own very quickly."

Eliza nodded.

"But — houses. Or forts. Surely there'd be some trace?"

"A wooden house, untended, would rot and collapse, and one good storm, such as the one that brought us here to begin with, would scatter the bits of it into the tangle of trees, or into the sea. A single vine could cover what little remained, in no time at all."

Eliza stared at him.

"You really think that's what has happened?"

"I told you when we started this discussion, and I've told you before, that I don't *know* anything," he reminded her patiently. "I'm merely theorizing. I do know that there were many islands in these waters that were used by the pirates — meeting places for their fleets, where they could hide out and divide their loot and, inevitably, fight among themselves. And many of the islands have been fought over, for one reason or another, grabbed by first one country and then another, only to be finally abandoned."

"But why?"

"Fought over, or abandoned, or both?"

"Both. If an island is worth fighting over, wouldn't it be worth keeping?"

"Not necessarily. This is the New World, Liza — things change here more rapidly than they do at home. That little island across the bay that we call East Island, simply because it's to the east of us and shields us from the rays of the morning sun — we might have been wrecked on that, instead of here. We might have found a spring, and some fruits, and planted a garden, and been happy, until suddenly we found we had outgrown it. So we might have moved over here, and in a few weeks, if we went back to visit, we might not find a trace of ourselves there, or have the slightest desire to return to it permanently. Instead, we have discovered this one, and its greater benefits and advantages. At first we thought this plank palace of ours was a pretty fine house, and in an excellent situation, but now we dislike having our rear wall back up to a blank precipice and feel that our Hill menaces rather than protects us. And we are already thinking of building a finer house by the silk-cotton tree.

"So it could be with the islands. There's something else, too. Supposing a peaceful colony were founded here, and a nest of pirates sprang up nearby, too close for comfort. The English or Spanish or Dutch who lived here would move to another island, or perhaps go back home, having had enough of the tempestuous life theirs had become. Or the settlement might have been founded because the island was on or near a shipping route, which for one reason or another was later abandoned.

If ships no longer put in for water and food, or to trade, the people would move elsewhere. You see, it could have happened any number of ways, Liza."

"But long ago?"

"Long ago," he said reassuringly. "Today the world is quieter, more peaceful. When folk find islands, they stay on them, build for the future, planning to keep them and make them more beautiful and prosperous. And that is what we will do with ours, Eliza. Wait and see." And almost as soon as he had finished speaking, he fell asleep.

Keep it, she thought. He means, live here forever! It was a prospect she still found difficult to face. If he intended to live here forever, why, of course, she did too, but — surely not alone, only the two of them? They would bring out her sisters from England, Amelia anyway, and perhaps Edward's sister Maria, who was her own devoted friend. And Edward's brother. And servants to help them, and many other people to live in houses all around them.

"Well, why not?" she murmured to herself, and she too went to sleep.

Build for the future, Edward had said. *Make it more beautiful and prosperous*. That was the way she saw their days after that. And if that's the way Edward wanted to plan their lives, she would adapt herself. Sometimes she let her work fall in her lap, and looked off into space. Awbury, so small, so quiet, so homely, so filled with talk and people, with the peal of church bells and the sound of carriage wheels on the yellow roads. She choked back the homesickness that welled up in her throat when she thought of it, and looked around her, almost with defiance, at the strange wild beauty of their island. Except for missing her father, her sisters, the friends she had known always, she found herself strangely content with this island which was so beautiful. She watched Edward at work, saw him pause now and then to enjoy the green and blue world around him. It was right. Odd, perhaps, but right.

She had, she felt, conquered her fears, and even the start which the finding of the belt had given her was, more or less, forgotten. But she continued to follow when Edward led, and she must assume some initiative. She must learn to do things on her own. An opportunity presented itself so soon after she made her new resolution that she almost didn't recognize it for what it was.

They had been at their plantation all morning, walking to it laden with bags of yams, coccos, and seed to plant, and with the implements of digging, as well as with their lunch. Edward had let her help him a little with the planting, although he still disapproved, he reminded her, of women working in the field, and afterward she had gone to their favorite spot beneath the branches of the enormous tree to prepare the noon meal. The basket, which had been used for transporting the roots and seeds, was caked with dirt, and she took it to the spring to wash it. It was their only basket, and used for all sorts of things, and she was unhappy when she noticed that it was wearing out. The reeds were broken in many places; there was evidence that one whole side would soon pull away from the handle, and she could see no way in which to mend it.

"Reeds," she murmured to herself. "We have plenty of reeds on the island. The sand around the Lake is filled with them. And although I never made a basket in my life, Edward never built a house either. If he can do the one, I can do the other." So, without saying a word to him, she made a furtive trip to the Lake's edge, gathered some rushes, and began patiently to teach herself to weave. Her first attempts were far from successful, and she grew furious at the ineptitude of her own fingers, but finally the hours produced some sort of skill, and when at last she presented to her husband an unmistakable, if somewhat crookedly shaped and unevenly woven basket, he was both astonished and delighted.

"You will never cease to amaze me," he told her fondly. "The prettiest girl in Awbury — a weaver! Well, fancy."

Edward himself was being inventive constantly. His next move was to braid together some lengths of rope into what he told her the sailors called a gasket.

"If this works as I hope it will," he explained, "I will be able to get coconuts from the trees without cutting the trees down, which is something I haven't liked to do. You see, I make two of these loops, and use them as a sort of stepladder, moving one after the other up the trunk of the tree as I climb on them. Next," he added, pretending to scowl at her darkly, "we will build a boat. I know, my silly child, you believe that will be my coffin. Or our coffin, perhaps. It will be quite safe,

I assure you. And furthermore, we are going to learn to swim, as we've always said we would. I'm going to move the staves out several feet into the water, so that, instead of having a small bathing pool, we will have plenty of room and enough water to swim in. Don't glare at me with those big blue eyes. No shark, or other monster of the deep, will be able to penetrate the fence of boards and attack us, you may be sure of that."

Eliza shrugged and meekly smiled at him, hiding her thoughts as well as she could. She enjoyed splashing about in the clear, warm water fully as much as he did, but she couldn't imagine learning to swim. And although, as he implied, they would be safe in the boat, supposing it capsized or sank? He seemed to think everything would be all right if they could swim, but what good would this ability to propel oneself through the water do a person if a shark, with its ugly crescent-shaped mouth, was handy?

As she worked on her second basket, and he plaited his ropes into gaskets, she asked him, "Edward, are you as confused as I am about that word 'cocoa'? The roots you planted, which are so much like potatoes, and the nuts we use to make that new chocolate drink we enjoy so much, and the big nuts you're going to get down from the trees with those things you're making — they all seem to have the same name. And yet they're all quite different."

He shrugged and said lightly, "I'm afraid that's something Mr. Dickinson forgot to explain to me, when he was attending to my education. But I'll do my best. For one thing, I do know that, although people *say* 'cocoa' when they mean 'chocolate,' the word is really c-a-c-a-o. Why that is so, I don't know, and perhaps I have it wrong, anyway. The root that we think of as our local potato is spelled c-o-c-c-o. As for the coconuts — I give up! I suppose the words are, or were, all Spanish once, and perhaps the English succeeded in corrupting them when they took them over. One thing I'm most grateful to the Spanish for, however, is their cocoa, or chocolate drink. And that reminds me, when I was planting this morning, I thought that there was a place nearby that would grow sugarcane perfectly — and in time we will need more sugar, as you know. Didn't we bring some stalks from Jamaica?"

"I'm sure we did, and unless I'm mistaken, I've seen them within a day or two," she told him.

He sighed with pleasure. "We're too fortunate, I sometimes think," he said gravely. "Things go too well with us. Still, I suppose much of it is compensation for our having been deposited here in the first place. And now, when you've finished that bit you're twisting there, I have a surprise for you. Do you remember that very first patch we planted with melon and pumpkin seeds, before we seized on the area near our tree for the site of all our activities? I walked over there this morning. Come look."

He pulled her to her feet and led the way to where Black Point ran into the lake.

"Ned!" she cried. "I don't believe it." She looked at the tender young plants with delight. "But it's been little more than two weeks."

"Mr. Dickinson, the source of all knowledge, was right again!" he exclaimed. "Things do grow amazingly

in this climate. Our pineapple top is doing nicely too.
I made a sort of cone of shingles this morning, to put
over it. I'm sure Limpy and Mab would find it much
to their taste, if they happened on it, and this will keep
them from dining off it sometime when we're not
around."

A little later, as they were walking slowly back to the
plank house, they were greeted by a familiar cry from
one of the hens.

"Edward, she must have started laying!" Eliza cried.
She darted past her husband and promptly found the
egg near the mouth of the cavern. "This is wonderful.
If we leave it there for a nest egg, we'll have fresh eggs
regularly."

"We don't dare leave it there," he commented, frown-
ing a little. "Fidele has every virtue known to man,
and he's a doughty iguana hunter and all that, but I
wouldn't trust him with a new-laid egg. He's far too
fond of them, as you know. I'll build a hen house; I've
been thinking of it for quite a while anyway, but now
I have the incentive."

"How our colony grows!" she exclaimed. "You build
one structure after another. What do you plan to work
on next, I wonder?"

"Since you ask me," he said with a grin, "I plan to
work on a trap of some kind, in which we can catch fish.
And then the boat. Or no, I have just had a thought.
We will build the boat first of all."

She wished that she could be as interested in the
building of a boat as he was, or as she had been in his
other projects. She was, she admitted to herself, if not
aloud to her husband, still afraid of the boat. What

could he know of building one? And even if he managed
to make one that was watertight and wouldn't sink, and
that he could propel in some way, how were they to be
sure that some huge fish wouldn't rise through the
water directly beneath it and tip it over, or that a wave
or sudden gust of wind wouldn't come along and cap-
size them? She had been punting on the Avon many
times, but there she could see land and people all about,
and the boats were large and sturdy, and built by men
who knew how to build them.

Perhaps he would tire of his task, or give it up in
disgust. She listened, as she went about her own chores,
to the sounds of boatbuilding, the sawing and the ham-
mering, down by the water's edge north of Black Point,
which came so clearly through the still air. Then came
the day when he enlisted her help in turning the awk-
ward-looking thing over — she was astonished to find it
fully twelve feet long and five feet wide — so that he
could caulk and pitch the craft. Thereafter, instead of
noises, she was aware of odors, as his pitch kettle stewed
over the embers. Once she saw him happily throwing
handfuls of sand inside the boat, explaining as he did so
that the sand would mix itself into the pitch, and that
was supposed to prevent their clothes from sticking to
it when they went out on the water. For the thousandth
time, she thought, she found herself whispering: "How
does he know these things?"

She would refuse to go out with him, that was all
there was to it. She had watched him in their little
stockade in the water, and he was indeed learning to
swim a little. If the boat overturned, he could at least

save himself. She had done her best, she really had, but she was sure she would never be able to stay on the surface of the water. In the shallowest part of their shark-proof stockade, where she could touch a toe or a fingertip to the sand, she could *almost* float, but not quite. So, if the boat tipped over, he would have only himself to save, if he were alone.

This was the first major cloud on the horizon for Eliza. Edward had said she showed courage throughout the storm and the early hours on the island, but that had been because she had had to show courage! There was nothing else to do. This required bravery of another sort, to step into the clumsy boat deliberately, aware of the dangers involved, knowing that she had only to refuse and then she could remain safely on the shore.

When the moment came, she faced it nervously. Her hands were clammy, and her stomach seemed to quiver. They had just finished their dinner, and she had known for some time that the end of the siesta would mean the beginning of the ordeal.

"Come, see my work of art," he said, holding out his hand and looking proud. He had streaks of pitch on his face, and the knuckles of his hands were black with it. She reminded herself that he had spent long hours at this work, and that she must give him her attention and praise for that reason, if for no other. It looked so crude and homemade, sitting there crookedly on the sand, she thought, watching listlessly as he tied a rope to the bow.

"Now," he said, "I'll lift the bow with this plank, and you put one of those spikes under the bow — Good.

And another under the stern. There, you see we have two rollers. I'll push, put this roller in front — presto! We have launched a boat, Liza! Now we'll leave her for a day or two, so that the wood swells properly. When we find she's tight, we will try her out."

Eliza nearly fainted with relief, and at the same time she found that she could laugh at herself. All of that getting up her courage for nothing! Two days of not worrying about the boat, perhaps even of getting used to it. She was so happy about the delay that she tackled the Monday chore of laundering almost joyfully, gathered eggs from the cave where the hens still insisted on laying them and put them in the henhouse Edward had built, and worked on her baskets, finding that she was becoming more and more proficient at the making of them.

Edward laughed when she told him about the eggs.

"How many do you have in your little store?" he asked.

"Ten," she said proudly. "All the hens are laying now."

"When you have an even dozen, why don't you leave the new ones in the cave, to see what happens? Perhaps we've been wrong about Fidele — maybe he won't disturb them after all. Twelve gives us enough for a start."

Even though she filled her time and her thoughts with everyday matters, there was still the boat. And on Wednesday, close to sunset, she heard the words she had been dreading.

"Come, Eliza, I looked at our craft this morning and found it as tight as though the Benson brothers had built it in their yard on the banks of the Avon," he announced proudly. "Let's go try it out."

She followed him, endeavoring to keep up with his long strides and feeling as though her feet were made of lead. She was ashamed and yet, at the same time, she believed that she could persuade him that she was in the right. "We should not risk our lives." "There is so much yet we do not know about these waters." "It is not necessary that we move about; we have too much to do as it is."

So many excuses, and not one of them sounded right, even to herself.

"That was a delicious stew you made for dinner," she said in a low voice, casting about for something to say that would please him. Actually, it was one more thing to be ashamed of. She had gone to sleep on the bed in the Tent, worn out from her morning exertions and from the heat. These sudden lassitudes were becoming more and more frequent, lately, and the ability to fall into a deep sleep without a moment's warning no longer astonished her. Sometimes Edward did too, but today he had let her sleep and had gone about preparing a new dish which she had found delicious.

"The omniscient Mr. Dickinson," he said cheerily. "As I told you, he called it pepper pot. We had it one noon when we were riding to the other side of the island, and stopped to visit a friend of his. It was simply a stew such as we were brought up on, meat and vegetables, although we didn't use salt beef for the meat or add capsicums to our stews at home. It was the capsicums, of course, that made it a pepper pot. Well, here we are, Eliza. Are you ready for your first maritime voyage since the storm lifted us across the reef and onto our island? Or would you rather I tried out this somewhat dubious craft myself, to make sure that she understands what is expected of her?"

Eliza clenched her fists. No, I am not ready, I will not go, she opened her mouth to say. You must go alone. Then she looked at the eagerness in his eyes, at the clumsy, ill-shaped boat he had worked so hard on, re-membered the stew he had made her just now, tired as he must have been, and she smiled at him.

"Give me your hand, Captain Seaward," she said, reaching out to him and putting one foot on the gunwale of the boat. "We are old hands at ships, are we not? And don't you think for a minute I'm going to stand on shore and watch you go adventuring all by yourself!"

CHAPTER 9

The Top of the Hill

AFTER THE FIRST few minutes in the boat, Eliza had forgotten to be afraid. It moved slowly and without grace as Edward pulled gently on his clumsy oars, but it moved and, because of its width, it did not rock.

As she said later, when they were on shore again and the boat was tied up, "There is one thing about this island. Nothing is ever what is expected of it. I didn't know, when we sailed on that voyage, that we were to be rained upon, and that the rain would be made up entirely of fish!"

That was exactly what had happened! After a few minutes of rowing about, while Edward got the feel of his oars and inspected the bottom of the boat carefully for leaks, he pulled in shore again, and telling her to stay where she was, carefully placed on the bow a tin baking pan filled with some substance he told her was a mixture of oakum and rotten wood. He set fire to this before he pushed off again.

"Wait and see!" he told her, laughing at her puzzled expression.

It wasn't long before the "rain" began. The mullet started almost at once to jump toward the light of the improvised torch in the bow, and within five minutes there were nine fat fish in the bottom of the boat. Edward, Eliza, and Fidele had been hit by the leaping mullet, and one had even fallen into the baking pan itself.

Edward had left the fish in the boat, knowing that there were no thieves about to steal their catch from them, and the next morning they had roasted the two largest for their breakfast.

As they ate them, Eliza again made her remark about the unexpected turn things always seemed to take on the island. Edward agreed, and said, "I'll go a step farther with that thought, Liza. Every evening when we've watched the fish jump, we've wished we had some way of catching them. Now we do, but we have too many."

"Too many?"

"In this climate," he explained grimly, "we can't keep fish longer than overnight. Remember the crayfish? The rest of the fish in the boat will spoil. Apart from the fact that we don't want to go out every time we feel like having fish to eat, it's a shame to catch more than we need. Plentiful as they are, it isn't right. No, I must devise some sort of conservatory to keep them in, a place where they may stay alive until they're needed. I told you I had plans along those lines. That will come next, and a trap for fish too, since we don't want a diet of mullet exclusively. Those down there are going to go into our garden as fertilizer. What are your plans today, Eliza?"

"I," she said proudly, "am going to do the ironing. No, don't look at me like that. It's true that I never have ironed in my life, but I've watched it done, often enough. And yesterday I found the flatirons I packed for St. George's Cay, and with a blanket thrown over the settle in the Tent for a smoothing board, I am ready to make the attempt, anyway. I promise nothing," she added hastily, "in the way of results. But I know one thing — I don't intend to have you stand there staring at me! So go on about your gardening and leave me alone!"

It had taken all morning, because of her lack of experience, but when she had finished at last, she was reasonably proud of what she had done. She sat idly on the bench in front of the plank house, waiting for him to come from the garden, and watching Fidele, who had stayed with her this morning and who seemed, after running to the spring for a drink of water, to be frisking about in an unusual way.

"Look at Fidele!" she said to Edward when he appeared, pointing at the dog with a smile. "He seems possessed. You'd think he was trying to tell us something. Do you suppose he's caught another lizard for us?"

"No, he'd be bragging about it aloud. Well, come on, let's go with him. I think that's what he wants."

They followed Fidele down the path to the spring and they saw what it was he had tried to announce to them. Limpy, their lame goat, was standing there proudly, with two diminutive kids beside her. They looked at the little creatures with delight, murmuring their pleasure to Limpy, and suddenly Eliza said, "Why,

Edward, look at Fidele. He's drinking water as though he hadn't had any for days. I do believe he came down and saw Limpy and her new family and rushed right back to tell us, without even stopping for his drink at all!"

One of the ducks had disappeared that day too, and Eliza was sure this meant that the duck was nesting, so what with the new kids and her hopes for a duckling brood, she was so pleased at their domestic situation that she made no objection the next day when Edward suggested they travel to the plantation near the silk-cotton tree by water instead of by land.

"Surely it's easier to transport all the tools we need, the food we'll eat, and your reeds for basketmaking by boat rather than over that rough path every day," he insisted. "Wait and see how much easier it will be this way. And besides, we'll see more of our world."

She confessed it was far more pleasant to sit in the stern of the boat while he rowed them slowly along the shore, and they found it interesting to look at the familiar landmarks from the other side. The journey by water proved to be about the same in length as it was by land, and it took about the same length of time, because of their leisurely progress. When Edward rowed around Black Point, they looked possessively at their Tree behind the sandy beach.

"It's beautiful, even more beautiful from here," she said dreamily, looking at the tremendous canopy, green with an elusive tinge of gold, spreading over the land on the slope above.

He nodded. "And useful," he agreed. "And somehow important. Not only as the site of our future home,

Liza, but it seems to be the focal point of our life here. I feel drawn to it, in some way, as though, like Fidele with the kids, it's trying to tell us something." He grinned sheepishly. "I suppose that sounds as though I'm daft," he admitted. "Doesn't it, Liza?"

She gazed up the slope at the tree.

"No, I feel something too," she murmured. "Perhaps because it's more like the trees at home, or perhaps . . ."

She left the sentence unfinished. She hadn't thought of it before, but perhaps the tree *was* trying to tell them something. Whatever it was, maybe someday they would find out.

This time, instead of climbing up to their usual spot, Eliza sat in the shade of a shelving rock on the beach, while Edward worked at planting Indian corn, shaddock seeds, and orange pips at the lower end of the garden.

"Everything in its place. Here our cornfield, there our orange grove," he said with a smile. "And, of course, up there our house."

He rested in the shade for a while after they ate, Fidele lying quietly at his side, but presently the dog became restless and ran away to kill an iguana for them, announcing his deed with his usual bragging bark. Edward went to find the prize, and came back saying, "I've found another spring, Liza. Or rather, Fidele found it for me, or perhaps the lizard did. Anyway, there's a spring here. We'll never have to carry our water here again. And this is important to our future plans too, Liza, because it means a water supply close to our Plantation House, and the fact that we can transport our materials by boat makes the building of it all the more possible. And *that* means we shall have it even sooner than we'd hoped."

Eliza looked at the eager face and the bright, excited eyes, and thought, But he does too much as it is. And now he proposes to build a palace! But anything that makes him look so happy must be right. So she said quietly, "Things keep on happening for the good, Ned. It's — frightening, in a way. But — but wonderful."

"Not the least of our blessings," he said, patting the dog's head as he spoke, "is Fidele. He not only catches lizards for us, and brings us news of blessed events, but he is learning to herd the goats and prevent the hens from straying. I've been watching him lately, and he has a true instinct for it."

"Probably," she said slowly, "this is a better life for him than the one he would have had in Awbury. Or at St. George's Cay. It's more like the life dogs were once born for, I suppose. And, Edward, I'm beginning to think perhaps it is a better life that we have too. If —" She bit her lip, wishing she had stopped in time.

"If we only had some companions," he agreed gravely. "There is always that, Eliza, and I think we shouldn't try to hide it from each other. But since here we are, and for who knows how long, we're still bound to make the best of it. And the best is very good indeed as long as we have each other!"

Because her husband seemed determined to reach the summit of the promontory, the one they called the Hill, Eliza decided on her most drastic move yet, as far as her clothing was concerned. She discovered, in a seaman's chest, a pair of lightweight cotton trousers and she put them on under her short dimity bedgown and tucked the legs into the canvas boot tops. With a long strip of red bunting tied around her waist, to shorten the bedgown even further, and her red-and-white turban, she looked, she thought in despair, more like a Turkish woman than ever. But Edward approved of her costume heartily, telling her it was not only practical but becoming, and since there was no one else to see it, she not only left it on for the rest of the day but very quickly became used to it herself. It was certainly true that, without petticoats, even the shortened ones she had been wearing under the bedgown, she could make far better progress as they climbed, and it was a relief to both of them not to have to stop to free her skirts from every thorn that seemed to reach out for them.

All the same, the going was difficult. Edward, hacking away savagely with his broad knife or with the ax, cleared as rapidly as he could a path through the dwarf palms, contending mostly with the thorny spikes of the broad-leaved aloes.

"It's taken me two hours at least," he complained, stopping to rest after a while, "and I haven't succeeded in extending this six-inch-wide highway more than about thirty yards. The Hill is only six hundred feet high, at a guess, but at this rate it will take us weeks to get to the top."

"Must we get to the top?" Eliza asked practically. "I admit, we'd have a nice view from there, but it seems to take more effort than it might prove worth."

"We will be able to get a better idea of the size of our island," he said stubbornly. "And that's something we must know, sooner or later. Besides, probably from up there we can discover whether or not our Lake is open to the sea on the western side as well as on the east. If it is, then there are two islands, and not one. And furthermore, it's possible that we can find some trace of the boat the men took off in. There may be a wreck alongshore. That's something we must *know*, Eliza."

From his words she realized that he now felt that there was absolutely no hope of their former shipmates' having survived the storm. She and Edward had, and there were but two of them, but they had the ship's stores to fall back on, and the men in the boat had had nothing. Besides, twenty or so men, supposing they had all survived, would undoubtedly range around the island, and sooner or later would have come across the Seawards, who had stayed more or less in one spot.

She knew all of that without being told, or at least she reasoned it out at last. She could understand, too, why Edward had said they must *know* about the boat. There was something disquieting in the thought of a group of men rowing a small boat out into a storm and not being heard of again. Edward was right, it must be confirmed, their unhappy finish. Proof was needed.

The next time Edward stopped working at the underbrush, he looked pleased.

"I saw a break in the side of this mountain from our boat yesterday," he said. "And although it was obvious enough that we'd have to scramble through this jungle for a while, I felt sure that the belt of undergrowth was not too wide, and that on the other side of it we would find rocks. And right now, just as I was about to give up for the day, I came onto that part of the mountainside. The going won't be easy, Eliza, but at least we can proceed. With caution, I might add."

He led her into a rocky ravine, and told her to watch every step, because the floor of the ravine was covered with broken rock that had fallen from the precipice over their heads, and that each piece was treacherous and could slide down the ravine, carrying her with it. So they moved on, carefully and slowly, until Fidele provided some excitement by barking furiously. They hurried to the spot where he was, expecting to see an iguana, since it was what Edward called his "victorious hunter" bark, but instead, they discovered an animal not much larger than the lizards they were used to, but curiously rolled up into a ball, like a hedgehog.

"It's an armadillo!" Eliza exclaimed in amazement. "I can remember seeing its pictures in a book on queer animals, a funny old book that we had as children. I was always especially fond of the armadillo, but I must say I never expected to see one in the flesh! Don't hurt it, Edward, maybe we can make a pet of it."

"Always something unexpected, as you remarked the other day," he murmured with resignation. "All right, Mrs. Seaward, if you feel the need of a bizarre pet, we'll try. For now I'll roll him up in this kerchief and hang him on a tree. He can't get away and it won't hurt him. Now, let's climb a little more. It's nearly noon, and there's smooth going ahead, and I think our goal is in sight."

She was infected with his excitement and enthusiasm, and they made the summit in a burst of speed that left them breathless. Panting, they looked around them with delight, and began at once to find the answers to many of their questions. Just below them was the Lake, and it was open on both ends, as Edward had suggested it might be. Ahead, and across this fine harbor, was another island rising to a central peak that was nearly as high as the one on which they now stood.

To the east and running northward stood the long bar of reefs that their brig had floundered through and across more than five long weeks before, and inside the reef and its rims of foam were clusters of small islands.

"How did we manage to miss so many obstacles!" Edward wondered aloud. "We could have plunged ourselves onto that rocky dome, or glanced off the sheer sides of that dark island there. Instead, we —"

She slipped her hand into his, awed as he was by the aspect of what might have been.

"We are on a peninsula, as we thought," he went on, in a more normal voice, looking around in a pleased way.

"As you thought," she reminded him. "I leave all that sort of mental labor to you, Ned."

He squeezed her hand. Then he took from his belt the spyglass he had brought. Slowly, carefully, he swept the shores and the islands, even the glistening rocks of the reefs.

"There is no sign of them, anywhere," he said, and there was finality as well as regret in his voice. "Of course," he went on, and she detected a false note of cheer in his tone, "they could well have been blown to the south of us, where we cannot see them. Let's go as far to the north side of the Hill as we can, keeping over to our right so that we can see the shoreline below."

There was no shade on the top of the promontory, but there was a pleasant breeze, so they were not uncomfortable, and they walked ahead steadily for a distance of more than a mile, according to Edward's calculations. Finally, as they reached the edge of the rocky top of their mountain, they looked down and saw the *Mary*, held fast in her narrow inlet, and their plank house.

"The *Mary* looks like a child's toy, made of a bit of wood, and the Tent could be a little box to keep trinkets in," Eliza giggled. "We are up very high, aren't we, Edward?"

"If you couldn't tell that from the exertions of the climb, you're in very good condition!" he exclaimed. "Yes, we're probably close to six hundred feet up from the sea. And now, I think we should go back."

Eliza suddenly felt very tired. It would be easier going down than coming up, she knew, but it would be wearing and almost more than she could endure. She stared at the tiny brig below, and wondered if she would ever reach the shelter of its cabin and the comfort of her familiar bed.

"You know," said Edward, in a tone that was much too spritely to suit her at the moment, "I think perhaps we can take a shortcut. You know the hole in the roof of the cave? If we can find a way through that, the rest should be easy. After all, we've worn the path to the mouth of the cave pretty well."

"I don't feel equal to finding a way through any hole in the top of a cave," Eliza snapped. "And don't tell me you're going to tie a rope around my waist and lower me gently to the floor, because I just — won't — have — it."

He looked at her in amazement.

"B–but, Eliza, I only thought it would be easier for you, so I —"

"I'm sorry, Ned," she said penitently, ready to burst into tears and fighting the desire to. "I didn't mean to snap at you. I guess I really am pretty tired. I didn't realize, in all the excitement, what a strenuous trip it was up here. And the ship does look *so* far away. But I'll be all right. Only, please — please — let's not try anything new. Besides," she added, "there's our new pet. We can't leave him in that hammock all night!"

He laughed, mostly with relief at seeing her cheer up, she knew, and she assured him, contritely, that she was all right and that he shouldn't worry.

"I'm a thoughtless oaf, Liza. Let's sit down and rest for half an hour before we start out. It won't be so bad going down, and we'll be there before you know it."

They found the armadillo still in the handkerchief, although he had chewed a hole in it, so obviously he had had some idea of escaping.

"Probably found himself swinging, when he tried to free himself, and that may have scared him half to death," Edward said. "And, in case you don't know it, he weighs quite a lot. I'll be just as glad to reach that boat as you will. Aren't you glad we don't have to trudge all the way back to the brig on our tired old legs, but can row peacefully around in our fine boat?"

"But you have to row," Eliza pointed out. "I only have to sit there, like a lady."

"I'll be using an entirely different set of muscles," he retorted. "These aren't tired."

He owned to being thoroughly exhausted, however, by the time they had reached their plank house. A new harassment, which was becoming more and more noticeable, had begun to annoy them every evening at this time — great clouds of sand flies swarmed over the land, and settled upon them to become viciously biting insects. Tonight they were worse than ever, so after quickly stowing away the remains of the food they had carried with them for the day, putting a piece of melon on the floor for the armadillo, who kept himself steadfastly curled up, and shutting him in for the night, they hurried back to the *Mary*. Although they had used the settle Edward built in the plank house for their noontime siestas, they had never stayed overnight on shore, and now, thanks to the sand flies, it looked as though they never would.

"Thank heaven," he said, as they shut the companionway door overhead and wearily made their way to the cabin, "those nasty little insects haven't yet discovered the ship. Let us pray that they never do. Eliza, I would like to ask a favor of you. I like your new Turkish costume. Not only because it's practical, but I — well, I *like* it. It is most graceful and becoming, and it somehow suits you. Will you please keep on wearing it? It is modest enough, and surely more appropriate to our life here."

She sank down wearily on the bed, unwinding her turban and smiling at him gratefully.

"I don't know," she said, "what I have done to deserve

such a tactful husband. All day long, except for the last hour or so when I couldn't think at all from sheer fatigue, I've been wondering whether or not I dare ask you if you could bear to see me every day — except Sunday morning, of course — dressed like this. It is so comfortable, you can't imagine. Now you've made it practically a command performance for me to dress *à la Turque,* as you put it! There's just one thing, Ned. Please promise me you will never tell Charlotte about it. She would faint, or have the vapors, I feel sure."

"It would be almost worth breaking a promise for, to see the indomitable Charlotte at a loss for words," he chuckled. "But, no, I promise you, Liza, I will never tell Charlotte. Nor anyone else, if you wish me not to. And now, let's put an end to an exhausting day. But think of what we have done, Liza. We have climbed our Hill and have at last seen our own private domain. Though I can hardly move, at this moment, I find it all very exciting."

"I do too, Ned," she murmured sleepily. "Did you ever think, when you told me about the worldly goods you would one day give me, and the property we would one day possess, that you would bestow upon me not only one island, but two?"

CHAPTER 10

The Treasure Tree

"IF WE ALL AT once see strange animals that we have never seen here before, how can we be sure we will not as suddenly see men?" Eliza asked.

Edward smiled at her patiently.

"Your baskets don't suit you, Liza, because you wish them to look as though you had just bought them in Bristol, although they look perfectly all right to me. And that makes you like a fretting horse, skittish and out of sorts and ready to shy at trifles blowing in the wind. I have told you, men build fires. Armadillos and peccaries do not. And men tend to roam around and are seen."

"Not," she pointed out, "if they want not to be seen. Like Indians, who you say can walk softly, and who have great talents for hiding themselves among leaves. We saw no armadillos until a week or two ago. And none of those dreadful wild pigs until now, and for all we know, they've killed our Fidele. He was so brave in attacking them, all forty of them, to protect us . . ."

"Eliza, Eliza, your fancies are running away with you," he said soothingly. "You are much too good a nurse not to realize that Fidele is not going to die. Not a bit of it. The peccaries slashed him with their tusks and tore his skin. They did not bite him, or it might be another story altogether. He's uncomfortable, but we've bandaged him well, and he will be perfectly all right in a day or two. There were fewer than twenty of the animals. You are right, of course, about thinking it strange that in our weeks here we've never seen any sign of such creatures, but don't forget that we were farther afield than we have ever been, and quite probably we intruded into their territory. After all, we've never been on North Island before."

She nodded grudgingly. They had taken the boat and rowed across the narrow inlet to the other island, so that they could look back at and admire their own plantation from a distance. The boat, as Edward had once promised, had given them greater mobility, and they were becoming so accustomed to these little excursions that Eliza found she looked forward to them and to the new sights each trip produced. On this occasion Fidele himself had stirred up the band of attackers, or perhaps had ventured into their home.

"If they live there, the horrid little creatures, they can come here," she said.

"Possibly. Although I remember being told at home that our domestic pigs can't swim, that pigs, in fact, are the only animals that can't. It's something about their cutting their throats with their sharp hoofs, I think, but I'm not sure. So perhaps these cousins of theirs can't swim either."

"Supposing they come after us again. They were ready to attack us, not just our poor little dog."

"We killed a good many of them, Eliza. You shot one yourself. I'll never cease to be amazed at you."

Eliza shuddered. "I never expected to shoot anything in my life," she confessed. "I was so frightened I don't even remember doing it. But those little monsters were coming straight for us, and — you had given me the gun only a minute before."

"You did exactly what you were supposed to do. But as I was saying, Fidele provoked that attack. I think he'll be a little careful about where he goes hunting after this. Like us, he's grown careless, I suppose. But if they're not goaded into attacking, I doubt they'll bother us. We won that battle, certainly. If that's what's stirred you up, Eliza, forget all about it. I tell you, there are no men on this island, on either island. There are no wrecks that we can see, nor is there any sign of human habitations, old or new. Please put those thoughts out of your head."

"You found the belt," she said sulkily. "You said yourself that meant someone had been here."

"A long time ago," he agreed gravely.

Eliza was ashamed of her mood, as she always was. Edward was of such an even disposition that it put her in a light so much the worse. With one of her mercurial changes, she jumped to her feet and announced, "You told me that when you were in Baltimore you had been given pumpkin pie, and that you liked it almost as well as apple pie. We have pumpkins. I will see if I can't make us a pumpkin pie, if you will help me work out a way to bake it."

They went to the brig together, carrying Fidele, wound in his bandages, in a basket, because neither of them was willing to leave him alone in his condition. In the ship's stores they found heavy shallow baking plates, and from her own spice cupboard, given to her by Edward's aunt, Eliza took cloves, because Edward had told her that exotic flavor was an important part of the pie he had described to her. Edward solved his part of the problem easily; as soon as she had filled one of the pie plates, he inverted the other over the first, and placed them both directly above the glowing embers he had made. As usual, the business of working together, and the fact of being busy, had teased Eliza out of her dark mood, and when, the next morning, she saw that Fidele was indeed not hurt badly but would have recovered completely in another twenty-four hours, she forgot to be frightened.

Edward, who had learned a lesson with the crayfish, had made up his mind to salt the haunch of one of the peccaries they had killed in the battle Fidele had inadvertently started, and he had decided to hang it up in the cave, where it was cool and dark. One morning several days later, he suggested to Eliza that they go to the cave to make sure the meat was curing properly. "I actually have something else on my mind than the inspection of the pork," he confessed on the way. "The other day I drove a peg into the wall so that I could hang the joint on it, and I thought there was a hollow sound. I haven't had a chance to go back and test my ears on it since."

After they had made sure the peccary haunch was still sweet and edible, he rapped with his mallet on the cave wall, but to Eliza the sounds seemed perfectly usual.

"Yes, I can hear that this one hasn't got the solid *thunk* of that one," she said, bored, "but I suppose it has something to do with the rock formation, doesn't it?"

"I suppose so." He gave up suddenly, put down his mallet, and they went back to the plank house, where Eliza amused herself for a time with the armadillo, whose name had lately become Señor.

"He just looks Spanish!" Edward had said, laughing. "Don't ask me why."

Señor had spent his first night in captivity in the Tent. They had closed the door on him when they went down to the brig to sleep, leaving him rolled up in his uncompromising circle, but in the morning they found that the melon they had left for him had been eaten. Edward had made a stockade for him by driving shingles deep in the sandy soil outside. Later Eliza had watched him for a while, and had seen him unroll and try futilely to push his way out. When he discovered it couldn't be done, he promptly buried himself in the sand and thus disappeared completely.

In a day or two, apparently resigned to his new life, he roamed around his stockade, nibbled at the food Eliza threw to him, and was just now beginning the first wary approach to the melon rinds held out to him between the shingles, although he still refused to get too close to her. He was an odd creature to look at, his head small, his tail long, and his body covered with scales. His forefeet bore long strong claws, and his movements were slow, except when a sudden fright made him roll himself into his protective ball. In that position of defense, nothing could be seen of him, feet, head, or tail; he was only a hard, round curl, like a snail, covered with overlapping scales. A bizarre pet, Edward had called him, and if ever pet he became, that's what he would be, Eliza thought, smiling.

"Very soon," she announced, dropping down beside Edward on the bench, "Señor will be eating out of my hand, I'm sure of it."

"As do all señores, my love," Edward said absently.

Now what is he plotting? she wondered, and promptly forgot about it as she went to prepare their evening meal.

The next day was Sunday, a day Eliza always enjoyed because it meant resting from their labors and a stroll on Edward's arm, and, strangely enough, because she knew she would be all the happier to return to busyness on Monday. She forgot all about the cave and the noises Edward thought he had detected, and he said nothing that would lead her to think he had not forgotten too, but on Monday, after they had eaten their noon meal and were resting in the Tent, he brought up the subject once more.

"I'm going to try it again," he announced. "There is something odd about that cave, I'm sure of it."

"Why do you bother with it?" she yawned. "What do you care?"

"Mere curiosity," he answered. "Well, no, it is more than that, really. I have it in my head that there might be a thin wall of rock at one point. If that's true, and if I can break through it, we might have a sort of deep cool cupboard for our food. The ledge we have been using, way at the back, and the wall it's on, where I hung the pork, is by far the coolest part of the cave. Think how nice it would be if we could extend that by a few feet, even in one section of the wall. I could fit the recess out with shelves, and we would have the 'cold cellar' you've been mourning!"

Eliza was delighted with that thought. To her, mere idle curiosity was time-consuming; but looking for a cold cellar, like the one at home where preserves and cheeses and other partly perishable foods were kept, that was important. She went with him gladly, carrying a candle to be used in the darkness, because the back of the cave was almost as black as it was cool. Edward had with him their strongest and heaviest hatchet, brought from the brig for the purpose.

For a while he tapped lightly, listening with care.

"Here," he said at last. "There is no doubt about it. From this point, where I knocked in my peg the other day, way over to here, is much thinner. The sound is entirely different when you listen to it carefully. Would you light the candle and bring it in, Liza? There may be some difference in the color of the rock, or perhaps we can find cracks in it, if we examine it closely."

She lighted the candle at the tinderbox and brought it in, carefully shielding its yellow flame with her hand.

"Closer," he told her. "Hold it up against the wall, because — Eliza! Look at that!"

"It — it looks as though the wall were made of stones that had been — put there," she whispered. "Edward! The belt! And the chocolate trees!"

He nodded grimly.

"Exactly. Wait here, Liza, I'm going back to the brig for a crowbar."

"Wait!" she squeaked. "Wait, in this place? Not for a minute, Edward Seaward. I'm coming with you."

"You may wait outside in the sunlight," he called to her as he ran down the path. "There are no ghosts outside the cave, if you're so sure there are some back there in the dark."

She saw that in her haste to follow him out of the cave she had let the candle go out, and with a look at his fast retreating back, she hastily lighted it again. Her thoughts were in a turmoil. An artificial wall, in their cave? What could it mean? She was sure that whatever was revealed back of those rocks, when Edward forced his way through, would be something horrible — skeletons, perhaps, in crumbling uniforms, because Edward had said the belt might have been a soldier's, with guns still held in their bony hands.

He was back on a dead run, carrying the crowbar exultantly, and she hurried after him into the cave, almost allowing the candle to go out a second time in her haste.

"Stand back," he said, inserting his crowbar into a crack she couldn't see, and throwing all his weight on the end of it. "It may crumble suddenly."

The wall did not crumble suddenly, however. He was forced to remove one stone after another, until finally he had opened a hole big enough to allow him to wriggle through it. In great excitement he threw the crowbar down on the floor of the cave, put his head and shoulders into the opening, and began to push himself through.

"Oh, Edward, be careful," she wailed in terror. "Don't you want the light?" wondering what she would do in the darkness of the cave without it.

"I have more light here than you have," he called back, his voice muffled and echoing. "You know that hole at the top of the cave? This wall goes up toward it, and then stops." He pulled himself through the hole, dropped to the floor, and turned around so that he could face her. "The sunlight is bright in here, and your stalagmites and stalactites are more brilliant than you've ever seen. They're sparkling, and — " His head and shoulders disappeared from the opening, and she pressed closer to the wall. He hadn't cried out, but he might have fallen through a hole in the floor and into who knew what terrible depths!

"Edward, what is it? What's happened? Where are you?"

He reappeared as suddenly as he had vanished.

"Eliza," he said, and his voice was taut with excitecent. "Eliza, come through quickly. Here, I'll help you. Quickly. Oh, can't you hurry?"

With his help she managed to scramble through, first having the sense to push her candle into a crevice so that they would have light when they returned. If, she thought, they ever did. The darkness of the depth of the cave, the shadows that moved fitfully on the walls, the echoes that responded eerily to their own voices, all taunted and threatened one part of her mind, while the other part forced her to get herself through the jagged opening in the wall.

When he had deposited her safely on the floor of the cave, Edward reached through and picked up Fidele, who was complaining fussily at being left behind, and Eliza looked around her. In an instant all her fears disappeared. The shaft of bright sunlight that entered the gaping hole in the ceiling of the cave fell on the long, sharp shapes of the icicle-like forms growing downward from the roof and upward from the floor, and they sparkled and glittered — emerald, topaz, rose, and sapphire in the brilliant rays. Speechless, she feasted her eyes on the sparkle and the subtle colors until Edward pulled at her arm impatiently.

"That hole is relatively new," he said. "Or there wouldn't be all those things, formed by dripping water over the centuries. The hole dries the place out, you see. Look, there is the heap of rubble that fell when the hole broke through. But stop staring so, Liza, and look there in the corner."

Reluctantly, she tore her eyes from the shimmering beauty around her and dutifully looked into the corner, where he pointed. The chamber of the cave was small, about six feet by eight, and its floor was covered with deep dry sand, except for the heap of rock he pointed out as having fallen from above. Beyond, well at the end of the room, she saw some symmetrical shapes that appeared dim to her after the dazzle of the sun's rays on the glittering crystals.

"What — what is it?"

He crossed the room as quickly as he could, impeded by the soft sand under his feet.

She saw him stoop over the objects, touch one of them, and then whip his knife from his belt and slash at the shape nearest his hand. As her eyes grew accustomed to the light, she saw that it appeared to be a canvas sack.

He put his hand into the rent he had made, then pulled it out. She heard a chink of metal and saw something gleaming in his fingers.

"Gold," he whispered. "Gold coins!" Then his voice regained its strength. "Eliza, we have found treasure! Sacks and sacks of it. And behind these bags there's a long box of wood. Heaven only knows what we've stumbled on."

She moved to his side and bent over his hand, looking at the coins he held in the sunlight so that they could see them better.

"Gold coins? Are they English? I never saw any like these before. But — oh, Ned," a combination of relief and excitement made her feel giddy for a moment. "How ridiculous this is. Here we stand with a fortune at our feet — and we couldn't spend a shilling of it, if we tried!" In spite of herself, she giggled hysterically.

He patted her shoulder absently, the way he sometimes patted Fidele on the head while he was busy thinking of something else.

"They are doubloons, I'm sure of it. And doubloons are worth a great deal of money, each one of them being worth well over a pound, perhaps twice that much." Then for the first time he appeared to have heard her, because he said, "We do not intend to spend all our days on this island, Liza. We'll go back to England one day, and think of all we can buy with our treasure! And when we come back to our island, we can bring fine furniture for our house, and that set of dishes you have always wanted, and the best livestock, and servants whom we will pay well. You will never have to lift a finger again, Eliza Seaward, and I am the first to admit that you have done a lifetime's labor in the weeks we have been here."

He filled his pockets with coins, helping her through the opening, and they went back to the Tent. Eliza listened in silence as Edward prattled on exuberantly about how much money there might be in all the sacks and the box, how much it would bring when exchanged in England, what it would purchase for them. It was all going too fast for her. The very fact of the treasure they had found seemed to frighten her, its existence on their island and its lying right there in the cave they had visited so often since the day they had first happened on it, seemed to cast a fearful shadow over her mind. Too, there was the dismaying thought of the man or men who had put the bags there and who had built up the wall to conceal the treasure. Strangers walking on their paths, picking coconuts from the trees she and Edward regarded as their own, sleeping in the cave perhaps, or building a shelter on the Ridge where the plank house was.

As soon as her mind had come to accept all of this, it turned in another direction, and she tried wearily to ponder her questions and phrase her doubts carefully so that she would not make Edward angry. He was off on a flight of fancy that seemed to her to have no relation to them, or to their world, but consisted of varnished coaches that could be transported by ship, of blooded horses to pull them, of a fleet of vessels to ply between the island and Bristol, bringing back English wools and Chinese silks and tea in exchange for rare woods and sugar and the island delicacies that would be so much in demand back home.

Back home, she thought. It was the first time in several weeks that Edward had mentioned going back to England with any degree of conviction. She had thought him inured, as she had nearly become, to living forever on the island, to never seeing England again. It was the money, she decided, the sudden riches. How they were to get there was not yet apparent, but Edward must go home to Bristol and to Awbury, to display the results of his adventure, to show the world his new-found wealth.

Still the question plagued her, and when at last they had reached the Tent and she was readying their evening meal, she looked over at him. He had spread his pocketful of coins out on the table he had made, and was studying each one carefully, almost reverently. Eliza squared her shoulders. Father always told us to get our bad moments over with as quickly as possible, she thought. I am going to make him angry, but it must come out sometime.

"Edward," she began, and her voice was low and controlled, "may I ask a question of you?"

"Ask," he said cheerfully. "It may cost you a doubloon or two, but we have lots of them. Ask, Eliza."

"Edward, this money. It doesn't belong to us, you know. Someone else put it in the cave. Someone else may come back here and expect to find it. Have we a right to take it?"

"You're worrying about the strangers who are going to drive us from our island?" he asked genially. "Don't worry so much about them, Eliza. I've told you there's no danger."

"No," she said steadily. "It isn't that, Ned. This money, which you are 'spending' so rapidly and with such enjoyment —" She stopped to smile at him a little, then hurried on. "This money doesn't belong to us. If we took it, it would be stealing."

"Eliza, come here." He held out his hand until she took it, then made her sit down beside him. "Listen to me. I'm no thief, and if I found a man's purse in the road, I wouldn't hide it under my shirt and run. You know that."

"Of course, Edward," she protested. "It's just that everything's so strange and so — so different here. But the laws are the same, I think, and —"

"They are, indeed, Liza. Let me show you something. While I've been enjoying the 'spending' of our money, as you put it, I've been looking at it very carefully. There, you see this coin?" He held up a shining golden round and put it in Eliza's hand. "Of this dozen or so I brought back in my pockets, this is the newest. See the date? It says on it 1670, and it has the head of Carolus II. Charles the Second — seems to me he was the King of Spain until 1700 or thereabouts, and he was brother-in-law to the magnificent Louis XIV, if I remember correctly. Well, even though he may have been on the throne up to thirty-four years ago, these coins were struck in the first years of his reign. See, 1670. Looks as though it had just been minted, doesn't it? Certainly it has never circulated through grasping, greedy hands, do you agree? There are others that look as new as this, and some that do not. And — *the most recent date is*

1670. Remember one thing more, Eliza. That belt up there —" He jerked his head toward the high shelf where they had left it. "That belt is in a well-aged condition. We agreed to that, didn't we? So, take the belt and the date on this 'new' coin, and what have you got? Treasure that was hidden away, probably fifty or sixty years ago. And furthermore, if it is, as I suspect, pirate treasure, it was taken by some rough and tough buccaneer who took it from a hapless Spanish vessel, no doubt, after he'd killed the rightful owners. You could hardly say it belonged to the pirate, even if he were alive — and he most assuredly is not — and it wouldn't be possible to find out which Spanish don or captain gave up his life just because he once owned or transported it. For that matter, probably a good many ships were seized and robbed to provide that treasure.

"Under the circumstances, possession is the only law there is. I'm sure you agree. And it's not only my right, but my duty, to preserve the treasure and to take it to England, when and if we get the chance. Now, do you see?"

She nodded. "I'm sorry I was so silly, Edward," she told him. "I thought — I should have understood all of that, without having it explained to me."

"You weren't silly, you were honest and honorable, and that is one of the many things I love about you. Now let's eat, then throw our daily chores to the wind and go back to find out what's in that box!"

His enthusiasm was contagious, once her doubts had been swept away, and Eliza found that she had no more appetite than Edward seemed to. They made a pretense of eating, cleaned up hastily, and hurried back to the cave and the treasure. Edward pried open the wooden box easily enough, and their dazzled eyes found that it was full of gold and silver objects, intricately worked — ecclesiastical pieces, sword scabbards and hilts, many of them lavishly jeweled, chains and earrings of gold, gold and silver ingots, and quantities of gold and silver tissue.

Eliza was especially thrilled with this part of the treasure. She could see herself wearing the long heavy necklace and using some of the stiff tissue on her finest costumes. She touched the folds of gold and silver lovingly.

"Isn't it beautiful?" she murmured. "I will give Amelia some. And Charlotte too, of course," she added hastily. "Really, Ned, it's fit for a queen. If, as you once said, we may have to go to Court to petition the King for our islands, perhaps we could give Queen Caroline a length of it. Or would she think that a paltry gift?"

"The Queen is a woman," he said gently, "and would be delighted with a length of your stuff."

They hovered over the chest, fingering and exclaiming over its contents, until it suddenly grew very cold in the room. As the last trace of the sun slid away from the aperture overhead, Edward put back the lid carefully, and they stole out of the dark, cool depths of the cavern and back into the warm, bright air.

When he reached the mouth of the cave, Edward stood still, looking toward the silk-cotton tree. Eliza, glancing at him, was puzzled to see an almost reverent expression on his face.

"That tree," he said. "I've always had a feeling about it, you know. As though it marked something. Somehow your eyes always find it, no matter where you are, down below on the shore, or up here. I think it was put there to lead us to our treasure. I know, Eliza, we found the cave before we discovered our silk-cotton tree. You will think I'm becoming soft in the head, and perhaps I am. But I think possibly the tree led the pirates up the slope from the water, and from the tree they found the spring, and from the spring they were somehow guided to the cave. I feel sure of it, Eliza, the Tree has much to do with our happiness, on this island and later. I believe it is, for us at any rate, a treasure tree."

CHAPTER 11

Five in a Boat

THERE WERE MANY times, in the weeks that followed their discovery of the treasure, when Eliza wished they had never opened the wall, and that the treasure either remained still hidden from them or did not exist at all. The even temper of their days was destroyed, apparently forever. They had been so filled with pride at their accomplishments, and so willing to accept their destiny before, that they had been content, almost happy, on their island. But now they — or Edward, at any rate — felt they must get back to England. The treasure, although it provided a delightful prospect of eventual riches, imposed an obligation on them.

First of all, they must care for it. The bags were thoroughly rotted away in many places, so new bags must be made.

"If you had any doubts about the age of our find," Edward pointed out, "this should rout them for you. The room in the cave is dry, and the sacks have rotted from old age, not from being damp and moldy." He had gone below in the *Mary,* and had returned with several lengths of canvas.

"Here you are," he said, after cutting them up with care. "If you can manage to sew these pieces into bags, I'll make wooden boxes to hold them."

He had already counted the contents of the first old sack, and had discovered that it held exactly five hundred doubloons. The other sacks proved to be of precisely the same size. Eliza diligently stitched until her fingers were sore, and at last she had finished forty new canvas bags. Edward's boxes held three sacks each. They put the sacks in the boxes — thirteen boxes in all — and replaced the coins, with the wooden chest that they had never again opened, in the cave. There was one sack left over.

"We'll take this up to the Tent," Edward said. "And let's seal up the cave wall again. Frankly, I'm sick to death of those doubloons *and* the bags *and* the boxes."

Eliza sighed with relief. She hadn't known he felt the way she did about their treasure, but had assumed that her own feelings about it had been accentuated by sore fingers and aching shoulders. It was good to return to their normal life. The crops had needed no attention for the last two weeks, and since it had rained lightly several times, the garden stuff was all growing nicely. The melons and pumpkins, in particular, presented a lush carpet of huge green leaves starred with big golden flowers, and Edward remarked thankfully that the vines would bear long before their original stocks of fruit and vegetables could be used up. The sugarcanes, which had been planted only two weeks before, were already a foot above the ground.

Edward had, sometime ago, made a fish pot of reeds and bamboo. He had constructed it like two mousetraps joined together, with trap doors at the outer, narrow ends, so that the unwary fish could swim in, attracted by the bait he put there, and could not get out again. As soon as his fish pot was finished, they had all the fine food fish they wanted, in addition to the mullet they could catch so easily in the evenings. Too much, he had said cheerfully, and he had set about devising a conservatory by partially submerging one of the brig's big water casks, its sides bored with holes, in shallow water. The fish pot supplied them with fish every time they pulled it up, and the catch was placed in the barrel, so that they could let down a line into the conservatory and hook a fat, lively fish whenever they liked.

After all this was done, and the work in the garden finished, there had been nothing to do except care for the livestock; Mab had had two kids too, and the hens and the ducks had hatched several broods of young among them all. Save for a daily feeding, there was little enough to do for their growing family. The Seawards had, therefore, spent all their working hours on the bags and boxes, and their thoughts had been all too constantly occupied with the treasure. Eliza knew that sealing up the wall would not remove it entirely from their minds, but it would help, she thought, and perhaps they could find more pleasant duties that would keep them busy and restore their contentment.

"I wish we'd never found the treasure," she muttered to Fidele as she listened to Edward pounding the last rock into place with his mallet. "Things were so much more peaceful around here before that day." Still, as Edward had explained, so far the time spent since their marriage had not made him very successful in the matter of providing for the future. He was, obviously, earning nothing. His uncle's ship had been wrecked, and with it the cargo that would supply Uncle Timothy with the profit he expected from the trip. There was no one in Honduras representing his uncle's company, or overseeing the cutting of mahogany to be shipped to his uncle's warehouses, and no ship to send the fine wood on. Although Edward could in no way be held responsible for the wreck of the *Mary*, its loss might curtail his uncle's activities for a while, and for all they knew, he would not feel able to hire Edward when they returned.

Taking it all together, Eliza was forced to admit that it would be very useful to find oneself in England again, with money in one's pocket. She supposed it was silly of her, and girlish, to desire the return of the peaceful days on the island and to wish the money had never appeared, and she promised herself that she would try to put the treasure out of her mind, and to pay no attention to Edward whenever he started to build castles in the air with it.

When the gold was safely sealed away again, Edward suggested a tour of their domain. She noticed that he put the spyglass in his belt, and knew that from now on he would search diligently for a sail, whereas before, he had not troubled to take it with him except on the day that they climbed the Hill for the first time.

The survey of their estate was most satisfactory, and when they returned Edward carried back half a dozen young pumpkins, not fully grown. These, he told her, he had eaten in Baltimore as a vegetable with butter and pepper and he thought she would enjoy them.

"One of the nicest things about our growing prosperity," he told her, "is that we can be reckless and try new dishes. We have plenty of pumpkins and can afford to rob ourselves of a few, even though they are a little small."

When they had closed up the plank house for the night and returned to the brig, he said, "I had thought, when the really hot weather came, we could sleep up there on the Ridge, in the Tent, where there would be more breeze. But I had reckoned without the sand flies. Our cabin is getting much too warm for comfort, these hot nights. I'm going to try something new."

She watched him while he rigged a hammock of sorts in the main cabin of the brig. Hammocks, he told her cheerfully as he worked, had been discovered by Columbus when he first visited the New World.

"The Indians on these islands knew what they were about, when they invented these," he remarked, trying out his new gently swaying bed. "No wonder Columbus' men took the idea back to Spain with them."

There was more air in the large cabin, and with windows on both sides they found that at night there was a pleasant circulation of the slight breeze. Eliza was happy with the new accommodations, pleased with the state of the livestock and of growing things, and found that life had returned to normal. She was less happy, therefore, when Edward remarked that he thought he would begin to climb the Hill regularly, to look out for passing ships.

"The winter storms are over," he explained. "More ships will venture out on the seas, now that March is half gone."

At one point, she reflected, she would have been overjoyed. But by this time she loved the island and their life on it, and looked forward with no pleasure at all to the unknown or perhaps upsetting events the spying of a strange sail might bring upon them.

Still, day after day, he climbed to the top of the mountain, and returned shaking his head. He was not unhappy, she knew, but he somehow seemed to feel that he had an obligation, because of the treasure lying at the back of the cave, to find a sail, to signal a ship to come and remove them from the island. And so the days slipped along. It had been the eighteenth of February when they found the treasure, and the end of the month before they had it hidden away again. Almost every day through March and April, they went to the plantation by the silk-cotton tree, moving materials from the ship to the open space nearby, because Edward was preparing to build their fine, new home there. Some days he did nothing to forward that venture, because the melons and pumpkins were ripening and must be picked, and soon, he said, the yams and coccos should be dug. The corn was ripening too. It was an abundance that grew before their eyes, and although some of the harvest was a little strange, and the fact of harvesting in April even stranger, they looked on the results of their labors with great pleasure.

In mid-April they prepared for one of their long days at the silk-cotton tree. They had just finished their breakfast, and Edward was getting ready to begin his first task. Eliza sat idly, her hands in her lap, as she looked out over the slope below, the serene blue harbor fringed with green, and the water beyond the other island sparkling in the early morning sun. It was her favorite hour of the day, clear and cool, with the whole world fresh and rested after the black, star-sprinkled night.

Suddenly she froze as she sat, too paralyzed even to point as she cried, "Edward! Look! In the Lake!"

He wheeled and stared with an expression of disbelief. There was a large canoe there, being paddled along slowly. It had just entered from the western end and the occupants, they thought, seemed to be looking for shelter, because first one paddle was raised to point toward the north, then another was leveled almost directly at the Seawards.

Edward reached for his pistols and put them in his belt, where he could reach them quickly.

"Probably some Indians, blown from another island," he said. "They look as though they don't know the harbor here, and they seem to be moving ahead as though they aren't sure where they're going. Hand me that napkin, will you?"

He tied the white square to her pike, and ran, with Eliza after him, up the slope to slightly higher ground, where the occupants of the canoe could see his signal more easily.

"They're afraid of *us!*" Eliza exclaimed nervously. "See, they're talking us over. Wait, Ned, I have an idea."

She plunged back down the slope again, and returned with a large melon they had brought along to eat during the morning. Then, holding it in her two hands, she tried to convey an invitation to them, as her husband continued to wave. The canoe had drifted close to the shore, and a syllable or two came faintly through the air.

"*Amigos,* it sounds like," Edward said. "And I'm sure that's Spanish for 'friend.' I'll try it, anyway, and perhaps I can make it sound like their word." He called out as loudly as he could, "*¡Amigos! ¡Amigos!*" and was pleased to see them paddle toward them at once.

"Edward," Eliza said suddenly, plucking at his sleeve, "my clothes! I can't stand here and let them see me like this."

"You must, Eliza," he told her sternly. "Your costume is odd, but not immodest, as I've told you before. And if you should disappear now, it might frighten them. You could be going for help, you know, or for weapons. No, you stand right here. Forget what you're wearing. This is very important, Eliza, and your costume, under the circumstances, is not."

She knew he was right. So, very self-consciously, trying not to think of her trousers and her short gown, she followed him to the water's edge.

"Cut some melon and give it to them," she whispered.

Edward shook his head.

"Hand the melon to the old man who is stepping out," he said in a low voice. And as she did, he himself took a clasp knife from his pocket, opened it, and put it, handle foremost, in the old man's hand. The man immediately turned and cut into the melon, quickly handing each of his comrades a slice. This gave Eliza and Edward time to look over the newcomers. There were two men and two women, along with a young girl who seemed to be about sixteen or seventeen. The man who had taken the melon was very much older than the rest, and it seemed that it was to him the others looked for advice, and to whom they addressed their questions. They were all darkskinned, like the people who worked for Mr. Dickinson in Jamaica, and had intelligent faces with fine, dark eyes.

"I'll take the men up to where the food is, and we'll bring it back here," Edward said to Eliza. "Will you be afraid to stay with the women for a few minutes?"

"Of course not," she retorted. It was soon evident that the women might be afraid to stay with *her,* she saw with astonishment, as they eyed her carefully and seemed to want to edge away after their men, but suddenly one of the women, the oldest of the three, broke into rapid speech, pointing and smiling, and Eliza realized that her trousers, which she had actually managed to forget in the excitement of the moment, had deceived the strangers, and they had only just now recognized her sex!

The food was brought down, and the five newcomers ate everything eagerly. From the way they seized the water bottle as it went the rounds, the Seawards realized they had been for some time on the sea, and had lacked drinking water.

"Your offering them the melon was more thoughtful than I believed at the time," Edward muttered to her. "Can you imagine how a slice of cool melon would taste to one who'd been thirsty for hours, even days perhaps?"

Eliza blushed with pleasure. The gesture had been pure impulse on her part, and yet Edward was proud of

her for it. She looked at the dark faces. The old man's
head appeared to be a large version of one of the carved
nuts that sailors brought back into Bristol, fashioned
during the days of boredom on a long voyage home, and
sold for a few pennies each. But it was a kind face, its
seams and crevices not grotesque but worn away by life
and, somehow, knowledge. The younger man, who appeared to be in his late twenties, had sharper features,
and his dark skin was smooth. The old woman, heavy
and maternal, seemed to be the most exhausted of them
all, but she kept a sharp eye on the others, as though
to protect them. The younger woman seemed, Eliza
thought, to be a little stupid; her brown doglike eyes
were fastened on her plate, with only an occasional
glance directed toward the older woman. The girl was
lighter in skin than the others, and she was excessively
shy, never having once looked Eliza in the eye.

And their clothes! Goodness, Eliza thought, we must
find something for them to wear at once. The dresses
of the women were faded and torn, and quite obviously
had often been soaked by salt water and dried in the
blazing sun. Only the older man had a shirt, and that
was sleeveless. She saw that one of the sleeves had been
torn off, and now served as a bandage around the ankle
of the younger man. She and Edward, she reflected, had
not, in spite of the buffeting they had received, been in
such a dilapidated state.

When the sorry group had finished eating, Edward
motioned to them to follow him, and by means of
gestures he showed them that he wished them to rest
under the branches of the silk-cotton tree. His pantomime was readily understood and all but the old man

immediately stretched out in the shade of the huge tree and fell at once into exhausted sleep. The old man, obviously feeling responsible for them all, sat down next to Edward, and they tried to talk to each other. Eliza listened carefully to the man's speech, but she couldn't understand a syllable of it, and by the frustrated expression on Edward's face, she knew he could not either.

"I'm sure he speaks Spanish," he said at last to Eliza. "Probably an island patois of some kind. The Jamaican Negroes had the same sort of inflection, as I remember it. Not that it matters. If they spoke pure Castilian, I would understand no better. Uncle Timothy often suggested I learn Spanish and French. How right he was, and how I regret having been too lazy to trouble myself."

Finally the old man succeeded in conveying his own name to Edward, and when Edward pointed to the sleeping man under the tree, he said another name.

"His own name is Diego," Edward reported to Eliza. "And the other man's is something that sounds like Shaver."

"Shaver!" Eliza exclaimed with a giggle. "Shaver?"

"Shaver," Edward agreed, and he laughed with her. "I think perhaps it might be his way of pronouncing Xavier."

"But Shaver!" cried Eliza, going off into a new fit of giggles.

Diego began to laugh too, not knowing just why, and at that moment Xavier, hearing his name over and over, woke up and looked at them sleepily, a perplexed expression on his dark face. Diego quickly explained it to him; he grinned briefly and with just a touch of pride, Eliza thought, at having been the cause of the gaiety. Then he fell back into his sleep. Eliza wanted to know the names of the women, but since Edward didn't ask, she thought perhaps he had decided two names were enough to digest for the moment.

"Don't you think," she suggested timidly, "that perhaps we should get some more food for these people? All they had, after all, was what we brought for ourselves, and they seem not to have eaten for some time."

He smiled at her in the way that always made her feel proud, and nodded.

"The old man probably needs sleep as much as the others, if not more," he said. "But I believe he feels it his duty to keep watch, as it were. Let's take him with us, so he'll know we're not deserting him." He picked up the empty basket and put it into Diego's hand. The old man nodded gravely, and followed them as they walked the familiar path up the slope.

Eliza watched Diego's face carefully as they reached the plank house. He looked at it in amazement, then turned in a complete circle, looking in every direction, with a puzzled expression on his face. Edward was watching him closely too, and said gently, "I think, Liza, he has just realized that we are here alone, and that this is our house. It hadn't occurred to me before, but for all he knew we were part of a great settlement of people, and had left town for a picnic or some such."

He made gestures to Diego in an attempt to show that he understood what went on in the old man's mind, and led him a few feet to a spot where the brig could be seen below on the shore. With more gestures he described the wreck and showed him, by driving a shingle obliquely into the sand, that the *Mary* was fast on shore. Edward pointed to himself and to Eliza, shaking his head and waving broadly around the island, to demonstrate that they had been the only survivors.

Diego understood immediately. He nodded his head sadly, took Edward's hand and shook it respectfully, and went to examine the plank house, telling Edward with gestures of his own that his work was to be commended. After that, they gathered together food, and Edward, with a twinkle at Eliza, baited a hook, put a rod in her hand and said, "Go and catch us a fish, Mrs. Seaward."

Eliza made a face at him, but she walked quickly to the conservatory and in an instant had a fine, fat fish on the line. Diego was so amazed that he appeared to be rooted to the spot for a moment. But he hurried to take the fish from the hook, his seamed face breaking into grins as he examined the partially submerged barrel and understood its purpose. When they reached the others he woke his sleeping companions, pointed to the fish and the basket of food, and broke into his slurred, rapid speech, evidently telling them about all he had seen and learned while they had been napping.

Edward, when the tale had been told, tapped Xavier on the shoulder and called him "Shawveer," which was as close as he could get to Diego's pronunciation of the name. Xavier seemed pleased at the attempt, and followed Edward willingly enough to a spot where Edward began to build a fire, motioning to Xavier to help gather firewood. One of the women came to Xavier's side at once, and Edward, pointing to the man and saying "Shawveer," pointed at the woman with a question on his face.

"Hachinta," they answered together, just as Eliza came up to them.

"Her name is Hachinta?" she asked Edward. "Let's find out the names of the others. I'm sure the older one is Diego's wife, and the other his daughter."

Diego's wife's name proved to be Rota; the daughter's Mira.

"Eliza, I promised you a maid of your own, as soon as we reached our new home," Edward said. "I'm a little late in keeping my promise, I admit, but here she is, and her name is Mira."

"Perhaps," Eliza objected, "she doesn't wish to be my maid."

"She has little choice," he reminded her. "These people are dependent on us now, and we must care for them and protect them. In turn they must help us with the work. Rota can do the cooking and Hachinta can help and do the housework too, I think, but Mira you may train as you please, to be your personal servant." He looked at the men as they built the fire for Rota, who had taken charge of the fish and was preparing it with Hachinta's help. "Thank heaven, Eliza, we have our food supply still, and that our crops are doing so well. If we had had seven mouths to feed in the beginning instead of two, we might not have been so cheerful about planting seeds and waiting for them to grow."

"You wouldn't have had to work so hard either," Eliza retorted.

"True. Have you realized, Liza, that we can begin Plantation House in earnest? Our Plantation House under our own Treasure Tree! But we must find or build quarters for these people first; then we can begin work on our own home. I think once again fate has been abnormally kind to us, blowing these strong, kindly people ashore just when we are ready for them and need them the most!"

"And we must find them clothes, as soon as they've eaten," Eliza agreed. "I've been watching them carefully, Edward. Rota knows exactly what she's doing when it comes to cleaning and cooking fish, and she put those yams on to roast as though she'd been doing it all her life."

"She probably has!" he reminded her. "She must be a native of one of these islands, you know. Oh, Eliza, I'm so glad that you won't have to cook our strange foods over our inadequate fire any longer. It wasn't for that sort of life I took you from Awbury, you know."

"You hardly planned this sort of life for yourself," she retorted.

"Not in my wildest dreams," he agreed solemnly. "Look, Liza, I think perhaps the clothes should wait until tomorrow. These people are exhausted and need a long night's sleep."

"But where? In the Tent?"

"No, we'll put some planks on the ground in that shed I knocked together to store vegetables and tools in. And they can cover themselves with their sail — it's a very thin canvas and will keep out the cold for this one night anyway. Mira can sleep aboard with us."

It wasn't quite sunset when Edward succeeded in conveying to the newcomers that he wished them to get the sleep they needed so badly, and showed them the shed where they could spend the night. Eliza took Mira by the hand, and led her away from the others. The girl, who was still timid but much less shy than she had seemed at first, followed her willingly enough until they reached the brig. Then when Eliza tried to pull her up the ladder after her, Mira balked. She pointed to the water and shook her head violently.

"She's had enough of the ocean!" Edward said, laughing, "and I don't blame her. The *Mary* is a far cry from that canoe they traveled heaven knows how far in, but it probably doesn't strike her as a very good idea to go to sea again." He touched Mira on the arm, pointed to the ropes that ran from the brig around the rocks and made a great show of trying to push the *Mary* out into the water, grunting and shaking his head vigorously, until she got the idea. She smiled, shrugged a little, and scrambled quickly up the ladder. Fidele, who had been tossed up by Edward before Eliza made the ascent, greeted her with a welcoming bark, and obligingly licked her hands. An immediate friendship had been established between Mira and the little dog, and Eliza felt that Fidele's presence on the ship had given the girl the last bit of courage she needed. They made a bed for her on the floor of the cabin, and she went to sleep at once, without even troubling to look around at her new surroundings.

The next day the new arrivals were given clothes, the men outfitted from the seamen's chests aboard, and the women from Eliza's own trunk and from lengths of fabric she had packed for gifts to such servants as she hoped to have someday. After they had all bathed and put on their new garments, they looked most unlike the tired, tattered lot that had arrived in their canoe the day before, and they were as pleased as children over their own appearance.

All the searching out of the clothes had determined Eliza to abandon her trousers, partly because she thought it highly unseemly to appear before strangers in them, and partly because there would probably be no more need for her to flounder through the brush after Edward. He had cleared away the paths that were used constantly anyway, and now, if he wanted to go exploring, he could have one of the men go with him. As for her, she need never worry about being left alone, since she had three female companions to help her, and to be her friends.

"I'm sorry to see them go," Edward told her, catching her folding up her Turkish trousers. "But I understand, Eliza. Our life here will never be quite the same again, I suppose, and although I think it's for the best, I will never forget our island paradise for two, and your place in it, as the sun and the moon and the center of my universe."

His speech brought tears to Eliza's eyes.

"We still have our island paradise," she said. "No one can take that away from us. But we won't have to work so hard anymore. Oh, Ned, what can happen to us next,

I wonder? The women are cooking and cleaning, the men are working in the garden and building themselves huts, and we —"

"We are going to be very busy just being happy," he said, kissing her. "And that's what we'll be — always."

CHAPTER 12

Plantation House

PERHAPS, ELIZA THOUGHT occasionally, smiling at herself and shaking her head a bit with the wonder of it all, perhaps there was less to do, because there were servants to help her with the household chores, and to work at house-building and in the field with Edward. But somehow it seemed as though they had more to do, each of them. Edward particularly. First he helped the men build quarters of their own, a wooden hut covered with canvas for each couple. Then he must hurry between the gardens and the plantation by the silk-cotton tree, where they were leveling land for the foundation of Plantation House, and the brig, where he gathered together tools and planks for the new home. It had to be Edward who found what they needed on the *Mary,* for he had made it a rule that only he and Eliza, and Mira, when she was accompanied by one of them, were allowed to go aboard.

Fidele was busy too. He had taken to the newcomers at once, as soon as Edward and Eliza had demonstrated that friendship and not fear was in order, and he accepted petting, food, and thrown sticks from everyone, regardless of language. Eliza hoped that the extra miles he covered in running from one friend to another would compensate for the numerous gifts of food, which she couldn't seem to curtail.

While Fidele had no trouble, Eliza found herself almost helpless in the matter of communication. Rota and Hachinta were able to cook the foods they knew, but the two women were not able to remember the simple instructions Eliza gave them whenever they were faced with a new dish, and she had to be on hand a great deal of the time. They were, as was Mira, more than willing to do what she told them, but it was necessary to tell them, as each task was completed, exactly what to do next. And this had to be done in pantomime, because of the language barrier.

As a matter of fact, it was the language difficulty that ate so viciously into their days at first, Eliza and Edward agreed, relaxing in the Tent after the others had gone down to their own quarters to eat their evening meal.

"Diego tries hard," Edward said, "and we have many words in common. But Xavier is perfectly content with my pointing to this or that or, if all else fails, to Diego's relayed instructions. And it all takes so much time!"

Eliza nodded wearily.

"I'm faced with the same problem," she agreed. "Rota acts as though she enjoyed my playacting. She sits on the bench, her face wreathed in smiles, and waits to see what I'll do next. I'm fair sick of it."

"I have an idea," Edward said. "Diego is willing to learn, and I'm sure Mira would be quick to catch your meaning. I will make a point of teaching all I can to

Diego, and you spend your time teaching words to Mira. In time, probably the others will either pick up English naturally, or they'll be ashamed because they're dependent on Mira and Diego."

After that, things began to go along more smoothly. Mira began to be very proud of her English, and Eliza was in turn proud of her pupil, but one day Mira's words startled her. They had been gathering together the soiled linen, to take to the creek. Eliza had told Mira that she wanted Hachinta to go with them, and her intention was that she herself should simply supervise this work today, so that after this Hachinta would be chief laundress.

"Clo'es read-y," said Mira proudly, standing in the doorway of the plank house. "Clo'es read-y, E-liz-a."

Eliza frowned. A servant should not call her Eliza! Then she realized that Edward always called her that in front of them, and that Mira was extremely proud of herself for having heard and remembered the name.

Eliza shook her head gently, smiling. "Not Eliza," she said, pointing to herself. "Señora."

"Señora," Mira agreed sunnily, and the moment was past. Later Eliza wondered if she had done right, and questioned Edward.

"Of course she should call you that," he said at once, "and not Eliza. Since it's inconceivable we should ever teach her to say Mrs. Seaward, Señora it is. They are not slaves, Eliza, but they are servants, and we must require respect of them."

One subject Eliza and Edward discussed frequently was that of the treasure. All except one bag of it was securely hidden behind the false wall of the cave, and

it was safe to assume that their people would never discover it, since they had little curiosity to begin with, and
were instinctively obedient. They were never allowed to
go to the cave alone, for one thing, but even if one of
them had gone there, he or she would never have
dreamed of investigating the rear wall. However, there
was that one sack in the plank house, and Edward was
afraid that Mira might one day, in her childish way,
start poking around in the little house and by accident
discover the secret of the canvas sack on the low shelf
under the window. One afternoon, when by prearrange-
ment Eliza was engaging all five of the others down at
the plantation, Edward removed the sack and stowed it
safely away in his trunk aboard the *Mary*.

The daily routine became more or less fixed, but
Sunday presented a new problem. It was impossible,
they knew, to explain to these people, with the few
words they could understand and with gestures, that
they were not to work on Sunday, so Edward and Eliza
decided to let the others have an outing, all by themselves, in the afternoon, retaining Mira because they
felt she would be little interested in a party of explora-
tion. First Eliza filled a large basket with provisions,
which Edward carried down to the canoe. Then, by
drawing outlines on the sand with a stick, by gesturing,
and finally by pointing to the sun, he made it clear that
he wanted the two couples to visit the other island, to
eat when and where they pleased, and to be back by
sundown.

"That may be the last we'll ever see of them," Edward
remarked grimly, as the canoe set forth.

"Oh, Edward!" Eliza protested. "They love us."

"They may love us, but I'm not too sure they know what it was we were trying to tell them," he explained. "For all we know, they thought I told them to row to the north and never to come back."

"Oh, Edward," she said again, reproachfully.

"I — I think I'm joking," he told her. "But we do have trouble communicating still. After all that business of getting the women down here, the men started to shove off without them, and yet I had been so sure they understood me."

"They're much too happy," Eliza insisted, "to think we're sending them away from the island forever. Much as they like food, they would know that that basketful wouldn't last very long. They'll be back, I'm sure. And after all, we would not have kept Mira here with us, if we had intended them to leave us."

"I know it and you know it," he said patiently. "And I think they know it. Well, we'll find out, in due course. I'm going up to the Tent and get the spyglass. It will be interesting to see what they do, once they reach the other side." He hastened up the slope to the plank house, then, with the telescope in his hand, rejoined Eliza and Mira under the silk-cotton tree. When he returned she had a new worry to discuss with him.

"Those awful little beasts that nearly killed Fidele," she fretted. "Those wild pigs. They might attack our poor people. Ned, we shouldn't have sent them there."

"Those awful little beasts were provoked into attack-ink Fidele by our little friend himself," Edward said, patting Fidele's smooth head. "I'm perfectly sure that they'll run as fast as their nasty, short legs will take them when they see four huge human beings approaching them. These are island people anyway, Eliza. They know what to expect in this sort of wilderness. Don't worry about them. Here, take a look through the telescope. You can see they're quite all right, and are having a fine time."

"I can't hold it steady," Eliza wailed. "It wavers all over when I try to look through it."

"I'll be ingenious," he told her, driving three sticks into the ground and crossing them so that they provided a rest for the telescope. "Now you can sit here and — wait until I get the thing focused — look, Liza, you can even see the expressions on their faces!"

The two couples had landed on the other side of the harbor, and were walking arm and arm up the beach. Eliza watched for a while and then gestured to Mira to come and look too. Mira approached the contraption timidly, squinted as she had seen Eliza do, and almost jumped out of her skin as she saw her father and mother, with Hachinta and Xavier, all but life-sized in front of her eye. Quickly she ran to the front of the spyglass and looked in, then ran back to see if the vision she had seen was not merely imagined. After that, still clearly puzzled, she watched the others gleefully, chuckling and murmuring to herself as they moved about. As those on the opposite shore sat down to their noon meal, Edward and Eliza pried Mira away from the telescope and took her up to the plank house, where they ate their own dinner.

The party brought back crayfish and some oysters, the first the Seawards had seen there, as well as some suckers of wild-banana plants. More important, they had enjoyed themselves hugely on their outing, and

Eliza realized how much a simple pleasure meant to them after their hard and faithful work. Since the first excursion had been such a success, Edward told Eliza he had another planned, so on the following Sunday Edward and Eliza again filled a basket with provisions, and by means of the gestures that still constituted the greater part of the island conversation, gave the four to understand that they would like to have them row around the isthmus, from the Lake to the *Mary*. As soon as the others had rounded Black Point, Edward beckoned to Eliza and Mira, and they hurried over the Ridge to the brig. They hadn't been there long before the canoe appeared around the cliff and came directly under the stern of the *Mary*. Then, unexpectedly, the canoe turned around and started northward, choosing by chance, for a stopping place, the rocky island on which the brig had first foundered. After a while the canoe was seen, through the spyglass which Mira had become so fond of, leaving the island, but for a long time after that there was no sight of it.

"But, Edward," Eliza said at last, "it's almost sundown, and you told them they must be home before then. You don't suppose something has happened."

"No, I feel sure they're all right," he said gently. "They probably were attracted by something and went farther than they thought, so that it's taking them longer to get back. Don't be so upset, Eliza, or your fears will be communicated to Mira, and we'll have a hysterical girl to deal with."

Eliza knew he was right, so she composed herself with difficulty. She hadn't realized how dependent on these people they had become, or how fond of each of them, and the thought of having, unwittingly to be sure, sent their friends to their doom she found unnerving.

It was Mira who spied them first, and they were rowing along the harbor from the west, rather than from the east.

"But they must have gone all around North Island!" Edward exclaimed. "Well, now we know how big it is. If they could row that distance, and not at any great pace either, and perhaps stopping now and then if they felt like it, it can't be more than a few miles around. We must go ourselves soon. It seems that we never have had time for lengthy excursions. But now we can see something of our world too."

Not long after this second Sunday excursion Eliza began to notice that language was becoming less and less of a problem.

"I think perhaps when they go off by themselves like that," Edward suggested, "they compare notes. If a word has puzzled one, perhaps another can explain it. Diego has a quick ear, and so has Rota I have noticed, or possibly it's because Rota is close to Mira, who has learned more English than any of them. In any case, we are getting so that we can converse without waving our arms around wildly all the time, and personally I find that a great relief. I must take them up to the top of the Hill next, Eliza, so that they can get an idea of where we are. In time they may be able to tell us how they got here."

In time, as he said, it came about. The work went on as usual day after day. For a while, all hands were busy with the harvesting, and by the end of the first week in

May, yams and coccos had been dug, the ripe melons and pumpkins gathered. The Indian corn had ripened too, and the storehouse Edward had built next to the Tent and in which the newcomers had at first sheltered, was filled with the first harvest.

"And we have another crop of everything well on its way," Edward told Eliza proudly. "It's hard to realize what big returns we get from relatively small plantings. It's truly a land of milk and honey, Liza."

Not much later, near the middle of May, the little colony found that it had entered the rainy season on their island. Each morning the day dawned fair and clear, but at about three o'clock in the afternoon they came to expect the clouds to gather and then to open up sending down rain upon them in a pouring torrent. After an hour or two of this, the rain stopped as suddenly as it had begun. This went on for a week, so the open spaces of the day were used to tend the livestock and, since the harvest was all in and there was nothing to do in the gardens, with a new task that Edward set for his men, to clear the cabbage palms from the high ground on the southern end of the silk-cotton plantation.

"As soon as this rainy season is over," he said to Eliza with great satisfaction, "we'll start our Plantation House in earnest. Right now they can finish clearing the ground when the sun shines, and take cover when the torrents begin. Besides, I remember Mr. Dickinson said that the top of the cabbage palm serves as an excellent vegetable, and I expect Rota will know how to prepare it."

When the rainy spell was over, Diego knew before anyone else what had happened. His women, without any bidding from Eliza, began to spread the linens and clothing that had been rained on and had never dried properly, and Diego himself, with his sign language, informed Edward that this was the time to plant. He pointed, by way of explanation, to the coconut trees around the plank house and between it and the beach which had grown enormously in the period just past. He and Edward between them determined where, in the next few days, the yams and corn, the coccos, the pumpkins, the melons, and other fruits should be planted, and the seeds were brought out of their store-house. By way of a celebration, Edward suggested to Eliza that they make a party out of catching a big supply of mullet by torchlight, and they were both much amused at the astonishment on the faces of their new friends. Eliza noticed that Edward was especially pleased. All too often he had planned a surprise or treat for these people, only to have them accept his efforts as a matter of course, indicating that whatever it was had been commonplace in their lives, wherever those lives had been led.

On the twenty-seventh of May, a Monday, and a date Eliza felt she would remember always, the actual work on Plantation House began. Edward had decided that Diego, with the help of the women, could finish the planting, and that Xavier was to be detailed to do the building near the Treasure Tree.

"He is a born builder," Edward said ruefully. "And frankly, I'll never forget the way he examined our Tent, and laughed at it."

"Oh, Ned," Eliza exclaimed. "I'm sure he didn't laugh."

"But he did. And of course he was right. In defense of myself," Edward added with a grin, "I will say that it is a most unusual type of construction for this part of the world. All the same, he looked it all over in great glee. But that is because he is a natural-born carpenter, and who am I to condemn providence for having sent me just what I wanted, at precisely the moment I needed him most. Now, Eliza, will you take one last look at my plans for our Plantation House?"

She had seen his rough sketch many times, but it had taken so much of his time and seemed so engrossing to him that she bent over it dutifully. The length of the house he had indicated as forty-four feet, and its depth was sixteen. The walls were to be fourteen feet high, and the interior was to be partitioned into three parts, a large room of sixteen feet, with two on either side, fourteen feet long.

It seemed to change from a crude sketch to an actual mansion in no time. In three months, the men created a recognizable house, its roof and floor, as well as the interior work, still to be finished. The plantation itself, under Diego's care, was flourishing with a new crop. And, as the end of August drew near, the language problem was nearly a thing of the past, except for an occasional word. By this time the five servants had been able to tell their story. They had been bought as slaves in Trinidad and had been shipped on a schooner to La Guaira on the Main. Two nights before they had paddled into the Lake, the schooner had struck a reef. The captain and his crew immediately took to a boat, appropriating all the provisions they could get their hands on, and left the slaves to die on the ship. However, there had been a canoe lashed to the deck. Xavier, with a huge knife, had cut it free and they had been able to launch it in the calm water. A piece of thin canvas had made a sail, and with only a handful of dried beans to see them through, the five frightened people had set forth just before the schooner sank under the surface of the water.

It had been their Hill, Eliza found, that they had sighted, the promontory that had seemed to the Seawards so menacing and frightening. Now it had served to guide these people to them.

"Lucky for us," Edward said later, "that it wasn't that captain and his crew who spied our Hill and made for it. Things would be somewhat different here, wouldn't you say? Why, Liza, we might be building a palace for him and his men. They might have tried to make slaves of us."

She shuddered, and said, "It's no good thinking about that, Ned. If we spent our time wondering what life would be like if things had turned out otherwise, we would never get our work done."

"You are wise beyond your years," he told her. "And speaking of years . . ."

She thought little enough of his unfinished sentence at the time, and even when she caught sly glances and heard little titters from the others at odd moments, she didn't add the signs together. Therefore it was a complete surprise to her when, on the eleventh of September, she found herself the central figure in a celebration built around her own birthday. Both Charlotte and Amelia, she remembered, had given small parties each year after they became young ladies, and she had looked forward to her own, planning the first of them this way and then that, but always with Edward at her side. Now she had him at her side, and they were eating Rota's lavish meal in surroundings she hadn't dreamed of at the time of her sisters' birthdays, and the friends who honored her were not the neighbors in Awbury whom she had known all her life, but five darkskinned people who meant more to her than anyone in the world except, of course, her husband. She looked overhead at the bright wheeling stars in the velvet sky, at the palm fronds moving and rustling in the light of the torches, listened to the fall of the spring as it played a thin melody against the background music of the eternal sea. What a magnificent way, she thought, sliding one hand into Edward's and stroking Fidele's warm round head with the other, to celebrate one's birthday!

Several weeks later, Plantation House was finished, and Edward and the men were busy for days unloading, from the hold of the *Mary,* the furniture that had stayed there all this time, the old family pieces and the new ones they had brought along for use in Honduras. With the furniture arranged in their new home, and a new storehouse completed, into which they moved all the remaining supplies from the brig, and where they would also house the fruits and vegetables from their bountiful gardens, the island could have been a bit of Awbury, set down in strange and colorful surroundings.

"Eliza, thank heaven you never wished to plant an English garden in this place," Edward had remarked to her once. "Many women would have insisted that such wildness should be restrained and tamed."

She had smiled to herself, thinking she would never tell him how often she had looked at the fragile orchids clinging to the silk-cotton tree, at the blaze and flame of strange, tropic blooms, and wished for quiet English roses and the orderly walks of an Awbury garden. But that was over; by this time the lush greens and riotous colors of the island pleased her eyes and filled her heart.

She was particularly happy to have her own pewter and crockery, her pots and pans, and the kettles and linen she had scarcely more than glimpsed since they left Bristol.

"It will be fun to sleep on land once more," she exclaimed. "And thank goodness for the screens Hachinta and Xavier have made us against the sand flies when they return. I do wish that we had brought with us our own bed, and the table and chairs we left behind because we expected to have them made for us in Honduras," she added, as Edward moved the bedding from the *Mary*. He had already placed at Plantation House the chairs and the small table they had used in the Tent. They looked crude and much too small in their new quarters. "But we could hardly foresee this!"

"We wanted to have them made for us at St. George's Cay because we wished them to be of mahogany," he reminded her, "and that was where the mahogany was to be found. But there are a few mahogany trees here, on North Island, and we have Xavier, who can fashion what we want in no time at all. We have everything we need, Eliza, or if there is anything lacking that I don't know about, tell me and we'll provide it, one way or the other."

"I know you will," she said humbly. "We have everything we need and much more."

"Next I plan to set the men at building a stone kitchen," he told her. "I'm worried about the dangers of fire with these wooden buildings we have. And the poultry has increased so rapidly, we've got to have a regular house for them. And —"

"There's no end to it," she said, laughing. "Every time you come to the end of some project I think, Now he will sit down and breathe for a bit. But that never happens."

"When it does, chances are I'll fall to pieces," he said. "Like sheds at home that drop apart from disuse. I'm happier when I have my hands busy and my mind pushing away at what's to be done next. I don't see you sitting around with your hands folded either, Eliza. I'm sure you're cut from the same cloth. Eliza, can you believe that Wednesday is not only Christmas Day, but that it marks the first anniversary of our deliverance from the shipwreck, and our arrival on the island?"

She had thought of it with wonder many times, remembering how desolate she had felt for the first few weeks when she had finally realized that their stay on the island was going to last longer than she had at first thought. How homesick she had been. Yet, now, although she longed sometimes to see her father and her sisters, she felt as though she wanted never to leave the island, which seemed to provide everything they needed for their happiness.

"I suppose it isn't necessary to warn you," her husband went on, "that the hurricane season is not yet over. We have been lucky enough so far, but there's no reason to think we'll escape serious storms altogether. Remember the one that brought us here, and prepare your mind and household accordingly. The men have their instructions, in case one should hit us, and let me show you the few things I believe we should do here at the big house, to make things secure."

The weather continued fine, in spite of Edward's warning, but on the fifth of January the sky became overcast, and the sea darkened to the color of ink. The wind gusted to hurricane force and finally brought with it the expected torrents of rain, but the little colony was secure enough, snug in their habitations, and with nothing to worry about. How different, Eliza thought, from the heaving deck, the flapping canvas and the screaming halyards of the other storm. She was nervous in spite of herself, and Fidele too seemed uneasy, refusing to be more than a few inches from her side at any time. Mira, on the other hand, paid no attention to the racket of the wind and the rain at all, remaining completely unconcerned.

At dawn, as the winds died away again, Edward woke up with such a start that he woke Eliza too.

"I hear guns," he said, "I'm sure of it." The men had heard them too, because they came running up to Plantation House through the darkness.

"Climb the Hill," Edward told them, struggling into his clothes, "and let me know what you see there. I'll be along presently."

Xavier came running back before Edward had finished dressing.

"Ship," he said. "On rocks there." He motioned to the southwest, indicating a considerable distance from the island. Edward hurried away with him, his spyglass under his arm. He returned a couple of hours later and told Eliza what he had seen.

"It was a brig," he said. "She had been caught on the reef, but was working her way off when I got there. Now she's gone, and just in time too, because I predict that another blow is in the making."

"Why did they fire guns?" she asked.

He shrugged it off. "I don't know, and never will, I suppose," he said quietly.

Eliza went about her work thoughtfully. A ship, so close, and to go away again. If it had sailed into their harbor, it could have taken them to England. They would come back to the island, of course, but now since their deliverance had been so close, she realized how much she wanted to go home, for a little while at least, to see her father and her sisters. There were so many things she could buy, too, to bring back to the island to make their life even more comfortable. Edward had expressed a desire for more farming implements, and they needed bigger kettles for cooking, tubs for washing, a smoothing board for her clothes . . . And she and Edward had many times discussed the possibility of bringing back other persons from home, to add to their colony. Amelia, she was sure, would want to come. Edward's brother John, who had always been taken with Amelia . . . Perhaps things had progressed with them, as she had always hoped, and they would come together, as man and wife. The Chambers brothers and their young wives, who lived not far from the Seaward place in Awbury — they would be fine company and good workers. A young family Edward knew in Bristol, who would, he thought, be glad of an opportunity to escape from a small farm where the ground was poor, to live in this land of plenty . . .

The near-rescue had affected Edward too, but in a different manner.

"We must now do something that we should have done long ago," he said. "If one ship can come so close to us, so can another. We must make a formal claim to our island, and we must fly our flag, so that anyone who comes here will know that this is not a bit of unknown territory, but an island that belongs to us and to the King."

So, on the sixteenth of January, 1735, after having carried the main topgallant mast of the brig up the Hill and planting it firmly on the summit, he hoisted the English colors to the top of his flagpole, saying solemnly, "We hereby take possession of these, the Seaward Islands, in the name of our sovereign King George II," followed by three cheers, crying, "King George and England forever!"

Eliza, unaccountably moved to tears, watched the colors flutter in the thin breeze, and felt that they were, somehow, nearer home. Strange, hot, green, luxuriant though it was, the island was at last a bit of England.

CHAPTER 13

Farewell to the Island

IT WAS THE SECOND week in February when they again heard guns, and from the summit of the Hill saw not one vessel but two, one a brig with Spanish colors flying, the other a schooner showing no colors at all. Eliza and the women were silent as they watched this battle taking place among the reefs, but Edward and the men left them on the Hill and went down to get as many firearms as they could carry, and some food.

"What do you intend to do?" Eliza asked him. The island army of three looked pitifully small, even on this tremendous vantage point, and she felt that it would be better for all concerned if they kept out of it.

"I'm not quite sure," he confessed, "but since the Spaniard is harassing the other, I am supposing that the schooner is English, and therefore I feel obliged to do what I can to help."

As it turned out, he was useful to the distressed schooner. He had fired only one shot when the brig hove to, and presently was seen as ready to leave the scene of action, possibly, as Edward pointed out, not so much because of the "garrison" high overhead, but because maneuvering through the reefs and small islands was too difficult for her. The schooner then answered Edward's hail and entered the harbor, anchoring just off Black Point.

"You always speak of our having come to the island through the back door," Eliza murmured, trying to still the small voice of fear that this new development had started up within her. "But so far, so has everyone else. From the east, as we did!"

Edward grinned and kissed her quickly, and then, calling to the men to follow, he hurried down from the Hill. Armed, Edward and Diego and Xavier paddled out to the schooner in the canoe and were, he reported later, enthusiastically greeted by the captain and his crew.

"Thank you," cried the captain, as soon as they were within hailing distance. "Your men on the height turned the trick for us. We were about ready to be taken by the *guardacostas* there, but you frightened him off for us."

"We're glad to have been of service," Edward told him as they drifted to the side of the schooner.

"What island is this?" the captain asked curiously, shading his eyes from the sun as he gazed about him. "I didn't know England owned any hereabouts."

"Nor does England know it yet!" Edward said, with a laugh. "Come ashore, all of you, and we'll tell you our story."

The women, with Eliza, had come down from the Hill, to announce that the Spanish coast guard vessel had gone almost out of sight. Edward sent Xavier and Hachinta up to the summit to keep watch, while he and Eliza, with the help of Diego, Rota, and Mira, prepared a feast for the captain and his crew.

As they ate, Captain Randall told them that he was an American, from the port of Norfolk in Virginia, that he had sailed, with English goods and with a half dozen slaves he had picked up in Santo Domingo, to Santa Marta, and was on his way home with cacao, when he'd fallen in with the *guardacostas*. He explained that his ship had been badly damaged on a reef in the fight, and that it must be repaired before he could go on toward the Chesapeake, where he had been headed.

Eliza listened as though in a dream. It seemed to her that she had heard it all before, that she knew Edward would presently bring up the subject of their taking passage with Captain Randall on the schooner, that he would agree and they would discuss the money . . . Perhaps she had imagined it too often, but at any rate, she knew that it would all take place, and that the captain and his ship had been sent here by providence to take them away from the island.

"The vessel must be repaired, first of all," Edward said. "And we will keep watch to make sure the Spaniard doesn't come back. I think perhaps he had a taste of the reefs out there, and of course he has no way of knowing that we're not a full British garrison. But we will keep watch, nonetheless."

That night the *guardacostas* did come back. Eliza, sitting terrified with the women, where she could hear but not see the battle, nearly fainted with joy when Edward returned to the house. He was tired and dirty, but proud.

"We routed them," he told her shortly. "We took two of their crewmen off, at their begging, I might add. They're Bermuda Negroes who had been pressed into service by the Spanish and wanted to be free. The others we told to take their boat and go. They tried to say that the schooner was smuggling in Spanish waters, and therefore they had a right to chase them, but I told them they were under the flag of an English garrison here, and not to let it happen again. They believed me," he finished, with a tired grin. "They have gone, and, I think, won't bother us again. Diego is tending to our two new hands, and I am going to go clean up."

So, with the addition of Jack Martin and Jemmy Purdy, there were now nine souls on Seaward Island, and all of the island's men had, in addition to their usual duties, the task of helping the captain repair his schooner. As a matter of common courtesy, the Seawards invited the captain to dine with them each day, and they always sent fresh fruits and vegetables, as well as fish from their conservatory, to the crew. Rota proved to be the sort of good cook who is pleased at having extra mouths to feed. She produced all her skills and favorite dishes for Captain Randall, even making for him the complicated dish Edward called "Rota's Yankee Pie," which took her hours to prepare.

At first they enjoyed Captain Randall's company, Edward in particular since he could talk with him about the Chesapeake and Baltimore, which Edward remembered with pleasure although he had been there but once. The captain was a short man, stocky, with blue eyes that were shrewd and almost crafty in a round, fleshy face. He had sailed to the Spanish Main many times in the last ten years, and he made something of a hobby of learning as much as he could of the Gulf of Mexico and its islands and surrounding shores. Day after day he regaled them with the stories he had heard of the area.

He was, it appeared, particularly interested in the pirates who had once infested these waters, and Edward led him on to talk of them. He was careful never to glance at Eliza, who had learned to keep her eyes on her sewing when the captain was there, for she never knew when the word "treasure" would be mentioned, and she wished to betray nothing to those small, cunning eyes.

"I firmly believe that our Treasure Tree served as a lure to a pirate ship," Edward had told Eliza. "Perhaps a band of buccaneers found our Lake once, seeking shelter from a storm, or perhaps from the Spanish, or even other pirates. And once in these serene waters, can't you imagine the leader looking up at the slopes and asking himself if there might not be a safe hiding place for his spoils? If I were down there in the harbor, looking at this island for the first time, I'm sure the enormous twisted trunk of our Tree would be the first thing to catch my eye. Then I'd go up the slope to take a look at it, and it would point straight at the cave.

"Of course, that's just a wild guess, but it could have been that way. We'll get our guest to tell us about the pirates and their ways, if we can do it without making him suspicious."

So the captain talked about his favorite subject, and they appeared to listen politely, as though they were fascinated by him rather than by his subject matter. He was a pompous little man, Eliza thought, and easily flattered. She thought him mean, too, and probably cruel — but he did know about pirates, so she listened.

Captain Randall's approach to the subject was from the opposite direction of Edward's, who found all pirates to be thieves and barbarians and worse. Captain Randall seemed to think of them as divine creatures, living in a golden age, and he obviously regretted the fact that he had been born too late to be one of them.

And he would make an excellent pirate, Eliza thought, stitching away, her needle flashing in the light from the fire and her eyes demurely fastened on her work. He has all the qualifications — greed and a sort of swaggering pride, and, I'm sure, great cruelty.

It was odd, she thought, that Captain Randall's talk turned so often to Henry Morgan, odd because Edward had spoken of him more frequently than of any other. Morgan was, clearly, William Randall's idol.

"Morgan was a genius," he insisted loudly, sprawling before the fire as though this were his own home and he alone in it. "A genius. His attack on Panama would have proved that, if nothing else had done so. The dirty Spanish thought the city safe from the attack from one direction, and so did not guard it properly in that quarter. Morgan saw the weakness at once, and that's how he took the place in the face of great odds. A genius."

"He might have made a good general," Edward said courteously. "But his tactics were brutal, and his treatment of his captives and his own men —"

"He won his libel suit, didn't he," the captain growled, "against the publisher who printed Esquemeling's lying account of him as an inhuman monster? Won

it in court, he did, and was knighted to boot, and returned to Jamaica as Deputy Governor as well. Ruthless
he may have been, but all brave men must be ruthless.
Disliked life ashore, and no wonder. When it bored
him he took to the sea as a man must do, and made a
glorious life for himself. As for the treatment of his men
— yes, he cheated them, and took more than his share.
He shouldn't have done that, I agree, but where would
they have been if it hadn't been for the old boy, eh?
They were lucky, you might say, to have served under
such a man."

"Some of them didn't think so perhaps," Edward
suggested.

"Morgan was the greatest of them all," Captain Randall continued. "He topped even that old Dutchman
Mansvelt, who for a time was the best of them all and
who was the first of the true buccaneers to cross the
Isthmus and see the Pacific. Pirate of Two Seas, you
might say. Mansvelt had the idea to set up a pirate
kingdom on one of these islands. Imagine that, a pirate
kingdom, and Morgan was to help him, but it fell
through somehow. Sir Henry Morgan was a great man,
in a great age."

"One thing is now very clear to me," Edward said
later, when the captain had returned to Diego's house,
which had been furnished him as temporary quarters,
with the crew using Xavier's. Temporarily the island
men were sleeping in the store shed and the women in
the hall of Plantation House. "Our friend Captain Randall is by nature a pirate himself, and I'm sure he believes that whatever gold and plunder that might be

found lying around belongs to him. I think we shall safeguard our treasure a little, Liza. I'm going to ask Xavier to build a barricade around the thicket outside the cave."

"But won't that point a finger at our treasure?"

"I'll tell Xavier and the others that having a dozen or more men work around here is a danger to our livestock, so to prevent accident to any of our fowl or animals, we'll pen them in, for the time being. I'll remove some of our provisions — they've been displaced anyway, now that Diego and Xavier and the new men sleep in the shed — to the cave, and that will give me reason enough to lock the door to the new barricade. The captain believes us penniless, I'm sure, and I intend that he should keep on believing so for a time, until it suits my purpose to tell him otherwise."

Sometimes Eliza grew a little weary of the captain constantly singing the praises of Morgan and his kind, but she knew Edward wished to learn all he could, so she forced herself to endure the long, dull hours of it. Once, however, he let fall something that jolted them both into stiff attention.

"No one knows," he said in his pompous manner, "where the island was that old Mansvelt and Morgan thought to make their headquarters. But I will know it when I find it, because there is a mark there, if you know what to look for. One of Morgan's men who came in once when his ship stopped off for water and wood took a look at a forty-foot rock that rises above a point of the island, at the entrance to the harbor, and he said, 'It looks like Old Morgan himself, that rock.' And so it was called. I had that from a man as shipped with me some years ago. He was along in years then, but he had been with Morgan and his lot when he was only a lad. Told me much, he did, but he was washed off the deck one night in a hurricane, or I would have had more from him. Still, someday I will sail into a harbor and see Morgan's Head, they call it yet, I suppose, and I will know where I am. And where I am, Morgan has been, and that could be a fine thing, because Morgan must have left his gold in safe places all over these islands, I think. And why not some of it where there is a huge rock as looks like him. Tickle his fancy, that would."

Edward skillfully changed the subject, and Eliza quietly took out the crooked stitches she had just made and put aside her work. Morgan's Head — she knew exactly where it was! It was on North Island, to the west, guarding the approach to the Lake from that side. The men had come back from one of their Sunday excursions talking of it, and Edward, curious, had gone with them later to see it for himself. He had been so impressed with the dark and towering rock that he had persuaded Eliza to take her longest sea voyage yet, and although she had not gone to the western side of the cliff, which Edward had told her was the most spectacular view, and where she could see the features of the giant face, she had allowed them to take her around a smaller point so that she could catch a glimpse of it from the back.

Supposing, she thought, Captain Randall took it into his head to look about him?

Fortunately, however, Captain Randall was uninterested in the rest of the island. He asked no questions, seldom looked around, and spent all his days supervising the work on the schooner, his evenings delivering his long, dull monologues on the prowess of pirates and how like Henry Morgan, William Randall would be if he had only had the opportunity. Edward had not yet asked the captain if he would be willing to take the Seawards as passengers when he sailed, but one evening after dinner, he spoke of wishing to return to Jamaica so that he could bring back skilled men who would help repair and float the brig.

"It'll be some time before you find a ship going to Jamaica," the captain said negligently.

Edward's eyes found Eliza's. They had discussed before the fact that they liked this man less and less. He had been genial enough at the start, when they had saved him from the Spanish coast guard ship, and he had been willing enough to eat their food and accept their hospitality. But as time went on, he had become more and more supercilious and condescending, and Eliza found his cold and careless remark to Edward distasteful.

"He should not talk to you like that" she stormed to Edward later, "after all you've done for him! Why would he act that way?"

"I suspect he thinks we're pretty small potatoes, Eliza," Edward told her. "We live on a pretty island, with five servants, now seven, it's true, and plenty of food that he and his men are only too happy to eat, but we are poor castaways, shipwrecked and far from home, and who would pay him for his trouble, if he should go out of his way for us?"

"You could buy his ship," Eliza said curtly. "But he doesn't know it."

"And he won't even suspect it," Edward said, "until he is ready to put to sea himself. Then we will have a little talk, Captain Randall and I."

"I don't like him. Is there something about ship captains that sets them apart?" Eliza demanded. "We didn't like Captain Molesworth, either. And now this one. He speaks of the blacks as though they were — animals of some kind. He asked you to tell our people they must help with the work on his ship. As though you could — or would — command them."

"Perhaps I could," Edward said reasonably. "I tell them what to do for me, and they do it."

"You give them their shelter and food and clothes and everything else they need," she protested.

Edward shrugged. "I told Captain Randall the men were free, and as far as I'm concerned they can leave me at any time and start their own homes on the island. It was plain he didn't believe me. But I did say that he could ask them if they would work for him, that if they agreed, I would free them from their assignments here, but that he must pay them for what they do."

"And quite right," Eliza agreed. "That man. I don't like him."

"Nor do I," Edward agreed. "But we are in no position to choose."

When the captain reported that his ship was nearly ready, Edward began to feel his way while Eliza sat by, sewing and listening.

"Where does your cargo of cacao go?" Edward asked. "I mean by that, to whom does it rightfully belong, and to whom must you deliver it?"

"A merchant named Dwyer, in Norfolk," the captain said.

"What price will you be paid?"

"I get so much for the trip out, and so much for the return," the captain said idly. "The ship is my own, and I am paid by the voyage. You can imagine how much money I have lost this trip, thanks to the Spaniard and that reef. It's cost me in time as much as a whole voyage."

Edward glanced at Eliza. His look said plainly, You were right when you said this man thinks of money above everything else.

"Do you mind," he asked courteously, "my asking you how much this trip to Santa Marta will net you?"

"It should be seven hundred dollars," Captain Randall said angrily, "but I expect Dwyer will pay me only six. Still, I made a little on the slaves I picked up and sold on my own. But this voyage, long as it has taken, won't give me enough to have made it worth my while."

They talked a little more, idly on the part of the captain, but with subtle purpose on Edward's. At last he made his move.

"If you will give up your cabin to my wife and myself," he said slowly, "and take us to Jamaica, which will not be more than a few weeks out of your way, and wait for us there a day or two while I see if I can buy a small ship to bring back here, I will give you half the amount you would receive for the round-trip passage. Agreed?"

"Three hundred and fifty dollars," Captain Randall said promptly, looking at Edward for the first time with interest on his crafty face.

"Three hundred dollars," Edward corrected him.

"I will think it over," the captain said at last. "And let you know this afternoon."

"He has gone to work out ways to ask for more money," Eliza giggled. "He could hardly wait to get away from us, to think it out. But, Edward, since you can offer him such a large sum, won't he suspect how you came by your money?"

"I saw the look of speculation in his little pig eyes," Edward told her with a grin, "as we were talking. He even glanced in the general direction of the *Mary,* and I'm pretty sure he decided my three hundred dollars came from the captain's chest, or perhaps represented payment for the mahogany the brig was to take back to my uncle. He did not suspect we'd found his precious Henry Morgan's treasure, for that's what I'm now convinced we did find, and I shall take great care that he doesn't."

"But the rock? Won't he see Morgan's Head when we sail, Ned?"

"Fortunately for us, the coast guard chased the good captain onto our reefs from the east. I think perhaps his ship could get through the passage from the Lake to the westward, and I'm sure the hazards among the reefs are fewer in that direction. I had wanted to prove my theory, but I will abandon that thought, and will tell him, if he asks, that the channel is too shallow for his schooner — and it may be — so that he will simply have to return the way he came. He'll get no glimpse of Morgan's Head, you may be sure."

That afternoon, when the captain appeared, she moved her chair so that he couldn't see her without turning his head. She had a feeling she was going to giggle.

"I have thought it over," he said, "and I would like to take your offer. But I am afraid that I should not, because it would break my charter party."

Edward looked at him in amazement, but Eliza for once couldn't hold her tongue. "You seem to forget that the Spanish coast guard would have broken your charter party, whatever that is, for good, if my husband hadn't been here to save your skin." She stood up angrily and flounced into the next room, not wanting to see his face or hear what he had to say.

"You flummoxed the poor fellow completely!" Edward told her later. "You should have seen him sitting there with his mouth wide open. But of course he couldn't do anything but agree, after your great speech! Parliament lost a golden tongue when you decided to be a woman, Eliza Seaward. He agreed to take us at my price, and when I said I wished to take one of the men with us and how much would he charge for his passage to Jamaica, he asked me almost timidly if ten dollars would be too much. I thought that quite a modest sum, and had been prepared to pay more, I admit. So I agreed, and offered to pay a like sum for Mira if you wish to take her with you. We wrote the agreement and signed it, each of us."

The preparations for leaving had Eliza in a whirl.

She had not thought there would be so much to do. It had been Edward's idea that if Mira and her parents were willing, they would suggest to one of the Bermudans that she marry one of them, and Mira, all bashful smiles and coy giggles, chose Jack Martin, who, when approached, was delighted. They decided to take the other Bermudan, Jemmy Purdy, to Jamaica, along with Diego. There Jemmy could find a wife, who would go back to the island with the others. Edward, as owner of the island, performed the marriage for Jack Martin and Mira, and told Purdy to prepare himself for the trip to Kingston. He then wrote certificates of freedom for each person on the island, so that if anything happened to him, they could prove their freedom to whoever might come to the island, and he and Eliza gave careful instructions to Xavier and Rota, who were to be in charge while the Seawards were gone.

The washing and ironing, the packing of boxes and trunks, all had to be done, and there was one event in particular that Eliza thought she would never forget. They waited until after midnight, then awakened Diego and Rota. The four, with Fidele, crept stealthily to the cave. Inside it, Edward and Diego, much to Diego's bewilderment, broke down the false walls. Rota and Diego looked without interest at the boxes lying in the hidden chamber of the cave. Eliza, watching their impassive faces, thought how different their expressions would be if the contents of the thirteen small boxes and the one larger one were to be spread out on the cave floor. How their eyes would pop at the sight of so much gold!

They worked until daylight, cording the boxes, marking each with a number and Edward's initials, and carrying them down to the plank house.

"Rota, thank you for your night's work. Please go home now and get your breakfast, if you will," Edward said at last, squaring his tired shoulders. "Diego, go with her, say good-by to the others, and then come back. As soon as he returns, Liza, you and I will have our breakfast, leaving Diego to keep watch here. I'll send Xavier to Diego, and they can carry the boxes to the schooner and put them in our cabin. Let us hope the captain is as busy with his own preparations as I think he is, so that he'll take no notice of our peculiar baggage. For a greedy man, he has very little curiosity, which works to our advantage."

After breakfast, Edward and Eliza walked around, looking at the familiar landmarks with nostalgia, as though they had already left them and were remembering them, instead of seeing them before their eyes. At last they hurried to the schooner, checked the boxes to make sure they were all stowed properly in their cabin, and went up on deck to say good-by to their people and their island. After they left shore under easy sail, Edward busied himself with taking soundings and comparing the sketches he had made of the island and the channels with the objects and landmarks around him, but at last he put the papers away and took Eliza's arm. She blinked her eyes rapidly, not wanting him to see that they were filled with tears, although she couldn't have said what the tears were for — whether it was unhappiness at leaving the island, or happiness at having taken the first step toward one day returning to England.

"Do you see that hummock there, to the south?" he asked her, motioning with his free hand. "That is our Hill, Eliza. And beneath it is our home, Plantation House, and all our people. And Limpy and Mab and their families, and the ducks and hens that traveled from Jamaica with us and went through the shipwreck, and *their* families. Though I'm not sure I can see it in this light, I think I can and I want to believe that I can, there is the canopy of our tree, our Treasure Tree. Yes, even from here it has that gleam of gold."

He put his arm around her and she moved as close to him as she could get, straining her eyes to see through the gathering dusk.

"When I think of our treasure, I don't mean those boxes below," he said. "The doubloons and the rest, they're going to ease our lives for us, there's no doubt about it. I'm not trying to pretend that I'm not glad we found them, and I do have great plans for them, I promise you! But to me the real treasure is the life we found on the island, every single golden day just as valuable a coin as the ones with Charles II on their sides. Every day, when we worked together and rested in the shade of our Tree, and every night when we felt we could reach up through its branches and pick stars like plums from the sky.

"And you, Eliza. Without you, there wouldn't be any island, or any treasure, or even any life for me. Without you nothing would matter to me. Do you understand what I'm trying to say, Eliza?"

She nodded. Her heart was too full for words. She knew what he meant, and if she had thought up the words herself first, she felt she would have used the same ones. She looked at the island, growing smaller as the schooner slid along smoothly in the glassy sea, and under the shade of their Hill she thought she saw the golden shine of the silk-cotton tree, its huge rounded top reaching out sheltering arms to protect them and their love.

"I can see it too," she murmured, so softly he had to bend to hear what she said. "I can see it too, Edward, our lovely Treasure Tree."

AUTHOR'S NOTE

Several years ago my husband and I flew from Costa
Rica to the island of Grand Cayman and looked down
with admiration and some longing from our great alti-
tude on an occasional island set like an emerald in the
sapphire *pavé* of the Caribbean. When, sometime later,
in an anthology of stories about buried treasure I read
the tale of the Seawards and the treasure they found on
Old Providence Island, off the coast of Nicaragua, I
realized that their island was probably one of those I
had seen and had been so enchanted with.

The story, of course, fascinated me at once. Who
doesn't long to be marooned on a desert island — and
on a honeymoon! I wanted to know more. I frantically
followed a sort of paper chase along the slow path to
the where, when, and why of the story, encountering
innumerable stone walls and lost scents, and finally
found a decrepit volume that was nearly a century old,
called *Sir Edward Seaward's Narrative of his Shipwreck
and Discovery of Certain Islands in the Caribbean Sea*.

Here I seemed to have stumbled onto a mystery. The
original edition said that it was "edited by Jane Porter."

Soon I discovered that in later editions the account is said to have been *written* by Jane Porter, in 1837. Which? The City Archivist of Bristol, England, where the great adventure began, very kindly sent me an article from the *Bristol Gazette* which calls the book "a literary mystery" and says it is not known whether the book was an actual diary, as Jane Porter claimed; whether it was the real or imaginary diary of her brother Sir William Porter; or whether Miss Porter invented the whole thing. If she did, her imagination was practically feverish; the most minute details of the day-to-day existence of the young couple were set forth painstakingly.

Apparently the "literary mystery" has perplexed many others. Nora Stirling, in the appendix to her *Treasure Under the Sea,* expressed her satisfaction that Jane Porter was in truth editor, rather than author, of the *Narrative,* and I am inclined to agree with her. Many times, though, in the process of digging and sorting, I have wondered whether I wasn't working on the wrong story, for it seemed that the enigmatic and mysterious Jane Porter, who wrote many fine books, including *Thaddeus of Warsaw* and *Scottish Chiefs* (this latter is said to have inspired Sir Walter Scott in the writing of his Waverley Novels), might provide equally interesting material, and that she, not Eliza Seaward, should be my heroine.

Still, Eliza and Edward and their island continued to fascinate me, and I stayed with them, following the meticulously detailed diary as closely as possible, saying to myself: How could an English lady in the early nineteenth century write such minute details of a tropical island, with its flora and fauna, if she had never

visited it? Why, in fact, would she bother? To me, a true
diary it has to be, and I have used it as such.

The island is, today, Old Providence Island, or Isla
de Providencia, while the original name, Santa Catalina, has been assigned to its smaller companion. Both
islands are owned by Colombia. Its history was one of
strife and change and excitement, long before the young
Seawards were blown onto its shores, and has been
touched upon briefly on pages 51–52, 128–129, 129–130,
215–216, when they speculate as to where they are and
in Captain Randall's conversation. The treasure that
they found was, quite possibly, hidden there by Henry
Morgan, although only the pirate ghosts who must haunt
the terrain could vouch for it.

I can't help wondering what those furtive ghosts
think when they see the happier shades of Eliza and
Edward Seaward, wandering hand in hand and so sunnily in the familiar places of their island paradise.

BIBLIOGRAPHY

Carse, Robert, *The Age of Piracy*. Rinehart & Company, Inc., 1957.

Cooper, Gordon, *Treasure-Trove, Pirate's Gold*. Wilfred Funk, Inc., 1951.

Corey, Herbert, "Across the Equator with the American Navy," *National Geographic* magazine, June, 1921.

Driscoll, Charles B., *Doubloons, The Story of Buried Treasure*. Farrar & Rinehart, Inc., 1930.

Encyclopedia of World History, compiled and edited by William L. Langer. Houghton Mifflin Company, 1948.

Gollomb, Joseph, *Pirates Old and New*. The Macauley Company, 1928.

Hart, Francis Russell, *Admirals of the Caribbean*. Houghton Mifflin Company, 1922.

Laughlin, Clara, *So You're Going to England*. Houghton Mifflin Company, 1948.

Masefield, John, *On the Spanish Main*. The Macmillan Company, 1925.

Oakley, Amy, *Behold the West Indies*. Longmans, Green & Co., 1951.

Ogrizek, Doré (editor), *Great Britain* (from The World in Color series). Whittlesey House, 1949.

Porter, Jane, *Sir Edward Seaward's Narrative of his Shipwreck*. London: William P. Nimmo, 1878.

Smith, Bradley, *Columbus in the New World*. Doubleday & Company, 1962.

Snow, Edward Rowe, *True Tales of Buried Treasure*. Dodd, Mead and Company, 1952.

Stirling, Nora B., *Exploring for Lost Treasure*. Garden City Books, 1960.

Stirling, Nora B., *Treasure Under the Sea*. Doubleday & Company, Inc., 1957.

Stockton, Frank R., *Buccaneers and Pirates of Our Coasts*. The Macmillan Company, 1898.

Wagner, Kip, "Drowned Galleons Yield Spanish Gold," *National Geographic* magazine, January, 1965.

MARJORY HALL has been writing something most of her life — majoring in English composition at Wellesley and writing editorial pages and booklets for the *Ladies' Home Journal,* advertising copy, a scattering of stories and articles — taking on whatever writing assignment has come along. The *Journal* job was in the Sub-Deb Department, and from that stems her interest in teen-age girls. After writing for them editorially, she ran a department-store promotion for the *Journal,* traveling around the country and visiting the stores where teen-agers congregated to see fashion and other shows, until a few thousand girls in the country were calling her Midge.

Because of the several years' experience as teen-age adviser, she wrote for a couple of years a twice-a-week column called "Talking to Teens" for the late *Boston Transcript,* and later turned to books of career fiction for girls. For several years she has been travel and resort editor for *Yankee Magazine.*

After many years in advertising as a copywriter and executive, she retired to become a free-lance writer and advertising consultant. When she is not traveling around the country on business, she is traveling outside it for pleasure. Her husband is a lawyer, and they live in a modern glass-fronted house on the edge of the ocean, which during the summer months they seem to be on when they're not in. Most of her life has been lived in New England, with a few years here and there spent in Philadelphia and New York.

(*Continued from front flap*)

natives fleeing the slave trade . . . and a sinister shipwrecked sea captain . . . make the story of their adventures even more exciting. By the time rescue arrived, their remote paradise seemed like home to Eliza, as she realized how "the lush green and riotous color of the island pleased her eye and filled her heart."

Adventure-minded girls will love the romance *and* the realism of this engaging tale.

THE AUTHOR

Marjory Hall, popular author of many stories for girls, began her acquaintance with them and their interests as Midge, on the editorial staff of the *Ladies' Home Journal* Sub-Deb Department. Later she became a copywriter, then an advertising executive, and still later an advertising consultant, before she married and retired to write young people's novels. She published many books of career fiction for girls—and then turned her attention to historical fiction. This is her fourth book in this genre. When she is not writing or working as an editor of *Yankee Magazine,* she is often traveling around the world with her husband. At home, they live in a glass-fronted house with a magnificent view of the coastline—on the edge of the ocean at Swampscott, Massachusetts.

Wisconsin State College at Eau Claire
LIBRARY RULES

No book should be taken from the Library until it has been properly charged out by the librarian.

Books may be kept two weeks, and renewed for one additional week.

A fine of ten cents a day will be charged for books kept over time.

In case of loss or damage the person borrowing this book will be held responsible for a part or the whole of the value of a new book plus processing costs.

DUE	DUE	DUE	DUE
MAR 30 '67			
MAY 8 '67			
MAY 15 '67			
NOV 2 '67			
FEB 15 '68			
APR 23 '68			
OCT 29			
APR 13 '71			